D1245264

NOUGHTS AND CROSSES

Scottish detectives investigate a murder

ROBERT McNEILL

Published by The Book Folks

London, 2020

© Robert McNeill

ISBN 978-1-913516-42-0

www.thebookfolks.com

This book is the fourth to feature DI Jack Knox. Details about the other books, and a list of characters, can be found at the back.

Chapter One

She was young; late teens, early twenties. Blonde hair, hazel-blue eyes; a pretty, oval face and well-proportioned figure.

He hadn't planned another conquest so soon, but an early evening meeting finished late and, feeling hungry, he'd dropped into Mario's Pizza Parlour on George IV Bridge.

He heard the other waitress call her Jan, and when she took his order, she gave him a seductive smile. He asked for a pepperoni and a Carlsberg Light, and after his pizza arrived he overheard a conversation she had with her colleague, a dumpy woman in her late thirties. The café was quiet, and he heard her tell the older waitress that she finished at nine. What piqued his interest, though, was how she got home.

'I room with another girl at Sylvan Place,' he heard her say. 'A short stroll via Forrest Road and Middle Meadow Walk. Only takes fifteen minutes.'

'Surely it's dangerous going via the Meadows at night?' the woman said. 'Wouldn't it be safer to take the bus? A 42 runs by there.'

Jan laughed. 'I know, Ellen,' she replied. 'But I enjoy the walk.'

Ellen shrugged. 'You know there've been attacks on young women lately? One at Portobello, another in Leith?'

'I do,' Jan said. 'But the Meadows are well lit. Besides, there are always folk about.'

He finished his meal, motioned for the bill and left a generous tip, then checked his watch: 8.25pm. He left the café and crossed to a pub opposite and ordered a shandy. Above the gantry a television was tuned to Channel 4+1, where presenter Jon Snow and a Liberal MP were discussing the impact of a no-deal Brexit. He feigned interest in the programme and sipped his drink, frequently glancing at his watch.

The television interview ended and the studio cut to a journalist at the Houses of Parliament, prompting him to check his watch again: 8.53pm. He drained his glass, left the bar, and walked a short distance to a nearby bus shelter, where he kept watch on the café entrance.

Several minutes went by, during which time only three people left the premises: an elderly couple and a male tourist carrying a backpack, who consulted a map before walking off in the direction of the High Street. Another few minutes passed and he checked his watch again, cursing inwardly. Eight minutes after nine. Had she already left? The place had been quiet, after all; maybe her boss had let her go early.

He dismissed the thought a moment later when he saw her exit and head towards Forrest Road. He followed, remaining on the opposite pavement, matching her pace until she passed Greyfriars Kirk, where he crossed at a traffic island and continued to shadow her.

He maintained twenty yards between them until she halted at the junction of Forrest Road and Lauriston Place, where the pedestrian lights were red. He stopped, affecting interest in a tobacconist's window until they sequenced back to green. She crossed and he followed, again keeping his distance.

What she told her colleague in the café proved true: there were dozens using the broad track which ran between Lauriston Place and the Meadows. He guessed a fair number were undergraduates, as this end of the thoroughfare was flanked on one side by Edinburgh University Medical School, and was a direct route through the Meadows to Marchmont, where many students rented accommodation.

Situated on the walkway's opposite flank was a luxury complex. Called Quartermile, it consisted of well-appointed apartments and offices developed on the site of the old Royal Infirmary.

Many of the walkers, joggers and people with dogs were likely to be residents of these apartments, he reasoned, which was why, even at 9.15pm, the thoroughfare was busy.

The human traffic thinned a bit when she reached the Meadows, a large park just south of the city centre. This section of Middle Meadow Walk continued to Melville Drive, a third of a mile distant. The park had few trees, and only a handful of pedestrians and cyclists shared the pathway. Still too many for his liking, he reflected, and, more importantly, not enough cover.

Melville Drive bisected the southern end of the Meadows, beyond which lay a narrow strip of greenery bordering its south-eastern periphery.

She was approaching a set of pedestrian lights at the junction of Middle Meadow Walk and Melville Drive when a bicycle flashed by him, moments later passing her and arriving at the lights, where its Lycra-clad rider thumbed the crossing button.

He took a mobile from his pocket and pretended to make a call, then closed in behind her just as an audible signal indicated pedestrian priority. The cyclist moved off and she crossed too, making for a pathway sheltered by trees opposite Fingal Place, a road running parallel with Melville Drive.

She glanced over her shoulder suddenly, prompting him to speak into the phone. 'I know, Nigel, I'm sorry,' he said, waving his hand in a gesture of annoyance. 'I was held back. I'm at Melville Drive. Be there in five minutes.'

It was fully dark now, and he was confident she hadn't recognised him, as she looked ahead again and continued on her way.

The mobile phone ruse.

He'd discovered it a month or two back when he was shadowing a girl in a quiet street in Newhaven. The young woman heard his footsteps and turned. Immediately anxious, she increased her pace. A pal rang him at that moment, and when he began talking he saw her relax. He came to the conclusion it was psychological: when she heard him speak, she assumed he was on his way to see someone and ceased to see him as a threat.

Even so, he'd had to dismiss her as a potential conquest when moments later a car stopped and an older woman picked her up.

But his latest target – Jan the waitress – *was* vulnerable. Right here, on this strip of pathway, the final leg of her journey. More, he was quick to identify the weak spot, which she now approached… a clump of bushes near a group of elm trees that obscured the view from both Melville Drive and Fingal Place.

Chapter Two

'Another one, boss,' Mason said. The young DC and her colleagues DS Bill Fulton and DC Mark Hathaway were seated at their desks at Gayfield Square Police Station and DI Jack Knox had just entered the room.

'Sexual assault?' Knox asked.

'Yes,' Mason confirmed and gestured to the phone. 'I was updated ten minutes ago. The victim's a Ms Ross, aged twenty-two. She's at St Leonards now with Sergeant Kate Lyall, one of the Sexual Offences Liaison Officers.'

'Where did it happen?'

'The Meadows,' Mason replied. 'A pedestrian pathway situated between Fingal Place and Melville Drive.'

'When?' Knox asked.

'Twenty past nine last night. Ms Ross works as a waitress at a pizza place in George IV Bridge. She was on her way home. Shares a flat with another girl at Sylvan Place.'

'How did she get to the path, Yvonne, did Lyall say?'

'Yes,' Mason replied. 'Via Forrest Road and Middle Meadow Walk.'

'Mm-hmm,' Knox said. 'She was able to identify her attacker?'

Mason shook her head. 'No. Apparently he was wearing a balaclava mask.'

'Forensics?'

'Ms Ross consented to an examination by our medical officer, and a semen swab was taken and sent for DNA analysis. We expect to find a match with the others.'

'Her attacker,' Knox said. 'Same MO?'

'Did he use a knife, you mean?'

'Yes.'

'Uh-huh,' Mason replied. 'Held to her throat. Neither of the other women reported him wearing a balaclava, though.'

At that moment a door to a room at the corner of the office opened and a tall uniformed officer exited. Detective Chief Inspector Ronald Warburton was a patrician-looking man in his late fifties. He walked to where the others were standing and addressed Knox.

'Morning, Jack,' he said. 'The Meadows assault, DC Mason's brought you up to speed?'

'Yes, sir. She was briefing me.'

Warburton pursed his lips and nodded over his shoulder. 'Another call just came in. DI Ed Murray, forensics. He's with pathologist Alexander Turley. More bad news, I'm afraid. A body's been found in the World's End Close at Netherbow. Male, early sixties. They're there now.' He shook his head. 'Looks like murder.'

Knox grimaced.

'I know, Jack, I know,' Warburton said. 'Never rains but it pours. You'll manage?'

Knox dipped his head in acknowledgment. 'Yes, sir,' he said. 'As you know, DC Mason's been assigned to the rape cases, so she'll visit St Leonards and join Sergeant Lyall to interview Ms Ross. DS Fulton and I will head to the Netherbow. DC Hathaway can hold the fort in case anything else comes in.'

'Good, Jack,' Warburton said. 'I leave it with you.'

* * *

World's End Close was a long, narrow alley leading off the Royal Mile near the junction of High Street and Canongate. As the detectives exited Knox's car, Fulton pointed to a group of brass plates inset into the road. 'These mark where the old Netherbow Port stood,' he said. 'In medieval times it was one of the gates that gave access to the city.' He nodded to the passageway. 'Which was how the close got its name. If you were an Edinburgh townie in those days, this was where your world ended.'

Knox gave Fulton a wry look and gestured towards the close. 'Apt for our victim, then.'

'So it would seem, boss,' Fulton said. 'Unfortunately.'

The pair approached a young uniformed policeman guarding the entrance and Knox flashed his warrant card. 'Forensics officer DI Murray and the pathologist,' he said. 'They're still here?'

'Yes, sir,' the constable said. 'Mr Murray and his assistant and Mr Turley. You'll find them near a couple of rubbish bins at the other end.'

Knox gave the PC an acknowledging nod, then he and Fulton walked to the top of the close, which opened into a narrow courtyard. Two large wheelie bins stood on the left, and three people knelt over a body lying in a prone position at the other side.

DI Ed Murray stood up as the detectives approached, and moved back a few yards. 'Morning, Jack,' he said. His female assistant also rose and stepped away from the scene. 'Warburton passed on my message, then,' Murray added. 'He was able to tell you much?'

'Only that the victim was a man in his early sixties,' Knox said, 'and you'd concluded it was murder.' Knox motioned towards the pathologist, who was still crouched over the body. 'Has Alex been able to confirm?'

'Yes. No doubt he'll give you the details himself in a minute, but it looks like the victim was dragged into the corner near the bins and suffered blows to the head.'

Murray's assistant, DS Liz Beattie, was a slight, red-haired woman in her early thirties. She went to a holdall placed at the top of the close and extracted a transparent evidence bag, which contained a fragment of house brick. 'Apparently, builders have been doing some work here in the last few weeks,' she said. 'They've a skip at the far corner of the courtyard.'

She held up the bag and continued, 'We think this was used to bludgeon the victim. It lay a few feet from the body. Part of clay brick, roughly twelve centimetres in length. There's blood and hair fragments along the broken edge, where it came in contact with the deceased's skull.'

'Good find, Liz,' Knox said, then turned to Murray. 'Any ID with the body?'

'A wallet containing several credit cards, a driving licence and £200 in cash... ten twenty-pound notes.'

'So the motive wasn't robbery?' Fulton asked.

'Doesn't appear to be.'

'The licence,' Knox said. 'Who is he?'

'Adrian Tuffnell, date of birth: 4/8/56. Address: 181 Marylebone Court, London. Mind you, I don't know if that's current. The licence is due for renewal in a couple of months, November. It's possible he hadn't got around to updating it. I'll check the licence for DNA along with the other items in the wallet and drop it off at the station later. Meantime I took a snap with my iPhone and sent it to your mobile.'

Knox took out his phone, glanced at the screen, and nodded. 'Thanks, Ed. I'll pass it to Hathaway when we're done here and have him check with the DVLA.'

Turley was a stocky, bearded man in his early fifties. He glanced at Knox, then left the body and walked over. 'Morning, Jack. Ed told you he'd identified the victim?'

'Morning, Alex,' Knox replied. 'Aye, he has. But so far we've only his age and address.'

'Uh-huh,' Turley said. 'Well, from appearances I'd say he was quite well-to-do. I'm going by his suit – the label says it was made by Gieves & Hawkes, one of Savile Row's top tailors. I believe he was carrying a fair bit of cash?'

'Yes. Ed tells me £200.' Knox indicated the evidence bag Beattie was holding. 'His attacker dealt him a blow with a half-brick. That was what killed him?'

'I'll be able to say definitively when I've completed the PM,' Turley said. 'But it certainly looks that way. He suffered a severe blow to the lambdoid suture, left side of the head, which appears to have resulted in a massive intracerebral hematoma – a substantial haemorrhage, in other words. Judging by stasis in the upper arm muscles, I'd put death at around 3am.'

'But the attack could have been earlier?' Knox asked.

'Definitely. Going by blood loss, I'd say two or three hours earlier.' Turley glanced back at the body and added, 'But there's something else.'

'Yes?' Knox asked.

'A strong possibility that, prior to the blow, there was an attempt at strangulation.' Turley paused. 'Marks on his throat indicate constriction of the laryngeal cartilage. There's some bruising to the left jaw, too, but that may have been caused if he was dragged.'

'Right, Alex,' Knox said. 'Okay if I give you a ring later, once you've completed the PM?'

Turley glanced at his watch. 'Of course,' he said. 'My assistants should be here any minute to pick up the body. I'll head down to the Cowgate with them and should be able to confirm my findings by noon.' He turned to Murray. 'I think Liz and Ed have completed photography and videography?'

'Yes, we have,' Beattie said. 'We were in the process of giving the locus a final check.'

Knox turned to Murray. 'Warburton didn't say who found him. Someone local?'

'Yes,' Murray replied, pointing to a block of flats at the top right-hand corner of the close. 'A Mr James Everett, flat 11c. Took his dog for a walk just before seven and spotted Tuffnell lying there.'

'Okay,' Knox replied. 'Bill and I will go and have a word. 'You'll let me know if you find DNA on the brick. Other than the victim's, I mean?'

'As soon as, Jack,' Murray replied. 'I'll give you a ring.'

Chapter Three

Sergeant Kate Lyall was in her middle thirties, five or six years older than Mason and had shoulder-length black hair, prematurely streaked with grey.

She was chatting to the female civilian desk clerk at St Leonards when Mason arrived, and turned and flashed a ready smile. 'Morning, Yvonne,' she said, then, indicating a vending machine near the reception desk, added, 'had coffee yet?'

'Morning, Kate,' Mason replied. 'At Gayfield Square, yes. Won't stop me having another, though.'

'Good,' Lyall said. 'Gives me an excuse to have one, too.'

Lyall took a small papier-mâché tray from a stand next to the machine, pressed a button, and a Styrofoam cup dropped into position and began to fill with steaming hot liquid. 'I take sugar, Yvonne. You?'

'Please.'

Lyall waited until the second cup filled, then placed both on the tray and nodded to a corridor leading off the entranceway. 'If you come into the office, I'll bring you up to date, then we can talk to her.'

'Ms Ross,' Mason said. 'How's she bearing up?'

Lyall made a face. 'Pretty traumatised. Only natural, I suppose, given the circumstances.'

She led the way to a small oblong room furnished with a table and two chairs, sat on one and put down the tray, then waved to the other.

As Mason took a seat and sipped her coffee, Lyall opened a foolscap folder and leafed through it until she found the page she was looking for, then read out the details of the latest assault.

'Just as well her flatmate's a nurse,' she said. 'Jan – that's our victim's Christian name – decided against reporting the rape and took a long, cleansing shower. She'd a change of heart afterward, but decided it was pointless as she thought we wouldn't find the attacker's sperm. Her friend, who arrived home an hour later, persuaded her otherwise.'

Mason nodded. 'I was wondering about the face mask. Neither of the other victims, Alice Cairns and Rachel Miller, said their attacker wore one. Do you think it's the same man?'

Lyall shrugged. 'That's something we won't know for sure until we get the DNA results.' She consulted the file for several moments, and added, 'Alice Cairns was grabbed at the foot of a stairwell in her block of flats and dragged towards the back door.' She paused. 'Hmm – she says in her statement that the bulb in the back stair was out. She was unable to see her attacker's face.'

Lyall flicked the page and continued, 'Similar situation with Rachel Miller. She was attacked a moment after she opened her front door. Pushed into her flat before she'd a chance to switch on the hall light.'

'Yes, I remember her saying that,' Mason said. 'So, there was no need for him to cover his face in either situation.'

Lyall picked up a pen and drummed it on the desk. 'Of course, he may still have carried a mask. Just didn't need to use it.'

'Uh-huh,' Mason said.

'I think we should re-interview the other women, anyway. It's a fortnight since Rachel's assault, nearly a month since Alice's. Fair chance they'll remember something else.'

There was a knock at the door, and a uniformed sergeant poked her head around and addressed Lyall. 'I've just taken a coffee to Ms Ross, Kate. Interview Room 2. Told her you'd only be a minute?'

Lyall stood up and tucked the file under her arm. 'Thanks, Jennifer,' she said. 'Tell her we're on our way.'

* * *

'It was Sandy who spotted him,' Everett was saying. He was thickset, balding and in his late sixties, and Knox and Fulton were seated in the living room of his flat at 11c World's End Close. Fifteen minutes had passed since the pathologist and the forensic officers departed the scene.

Everett's wife had just brought in a tray with a pot of tea and a plate of digestive biscuits, which she set down on a coffee table, inviting the detectives to help themselves.

'Your dog, you mean?' Knox said, pointing to a long-haired Jack Russell sitting at Everett's feet who, like Fulton, was eying the biscuits with interest.

'Yes,' Everett replied. 'I take him for a walk around seven, before the wife and I have breakfast.'

'Go on,' Knox said.

'Well, I never noticed anything out of the ordinary, but then it wasn't fully light. Sandy disappeared behind one of the bins and barked when I called him. At first, I thought he'd spotted a longtail – the rubbish attracts them.

'So, I called again, but he remained at the other side the bin. I was annoyed he wasn't paying any heed, and went over. Then I saw the body lying there. I came back upstairs and called the police straightaway.'

'I see,' Knox said. 'Do you walk your dog at night?'

Everett studied Knox for a long moment. 'Late at night, you mean?'

'No, not necessarily,' Knox replied. 'Before you retire.'

'Oh, I understand. You're wondering if I saw anything?'

'Yes.'

'Sorry, no. I usually take Sandy out at eleven-thirty or so; same last night. Never passed anyone in the close. The High Street was busy, though – even though the Festival's finished there are always tourists about. We walked down St Mary's Street to the foot of the Pleasance. There's a wee strip of greenery there Sandy likes to run around in. I like to think I'm responsible, though. Always carry a poop scoop and pick up his doings afterward.' He shook his head. 'Some buggers don't give a damn, let their dogs shit all over the place.'

'Jim!' Everett's diminutive wife walked back from the kitchen at that moment and directed an admonitory nod at her husband. 'Mind your language.'

'Sorry, Margaret,' Everett said sheepishly.

'And when you came back you saw no one, either?' Knox asked.

'No, not a soul.'

'You're on the first floor here,' Knox said. 'Are you able to hear folk entering or leaving the close?'

Mrs Everett sat down in an armchair opposite her husband. 'Quite often,' she said. 'Mostly it's not other residents, though.'

'Aye,' her husband chipped in. 'Strangers. Tourists touting cameras and iPhones, fascinated by the close name. They wander in and out, see if there's anything worth taking a photo of.'

Mrs Everett sniffed. 'Other times – late at night – it's courting couples.'

'Aye,' her husband said. 'No need to mention what they get up to.'

Mrs Everett shot her husband a hostile glance and he immediately looked abashed.

'You didn't hear anything last night,' Knox asked. 'Around midnight?'

'Can't say I did,' Everett said. 'You, Margaret?'

'I don't think so,' his wife replied. 'There are always a few drunks, of course. Once the pubs empty you can hear them going up and down the High Street, shouting and singing. More at weekends, though. Not Mondays.'

'Wait,' Everett said. 'There *was* something, just after twelve – I remember checking the time. I'd got up to use the toilet, when Sandy left his basket, ran to the door, and began growling. At first, I thought it was something in the High Street; you know how keen a dog's hearing can be. Then I heard it myself: like one of the bins being moved, followed by a sound like a stone hitting the ground. Then it went quiet again. I waited another minute or so, but heard nothing else. Neither did Sandy, apparently; he went back to his basket.'

'Funny,' his wife said. 'You never mentioned that to me.'

'You were asleep, Margaret, I didn't want to disturb you. Besides, I never gave it another thought. Until now.'

Chapter Four

Jan Ross glanced up as Lyall and Mason entered the room. The girl's face looked pale and drawn; her eyes red and puffy. 'Sorry to keep you, Jan,' Lyall said, then indicated a polystyrene cup on the table and added, 'The sergeant brought you some fresh coffee?'

'Yes, thank you,' Ross said.

Lyall sat down opposite and nodded towards Mason. 'This is my colleague, Yvonne.'

'Hello, Jan,' Mason said, taking a seat alongside Lyall.

'Hi.'

'We'd like to ask some questions, Jan,' Lyall said. 'I know you've been here for a couple of hours and are no doubt anxious to get home, but I promise we won't take long. Is that okay?'

'I told you what happened when I was brought here. Before I–' she hesitated, stifling a sob. 'Before I saw the doctor.'

'I know,' Lyall said, then indicated a NEAL recording machine on the table. 'But this interview is for our records.' She paused. 'You don't mind?'

Ross shook her head. 'No.'

'Good,' Lyall said, then opened the folder, glanced at her notes, and switched on the recorder. 'Interview between Ms Jan Ross and DS Kate Lyall and DC Yvonne Mason. Tuesday 10 September, 9.44am.

'Jan, you told me earlier you were raped on the pathway running between Melville Drive and Fingal Place at approximately 9.25pm. Is that correct?'

Ross stared at her coffee cup, but said nothing.

'Jan?' Lyall said.

Ross rolled her shoulders and gave a long sigh. 'Yes,' she replied.

'Look, Jan,' Lyall said, 'I know this is difficult, but I promise all the questions we'll ask are necessary, and anything you tell us is confidential and will only be used to help apprehend the man – you understand?'

'Yes,' Ross said.

'The place on the path where you were assaulted,' Mason said gently, 'could you describe it for us?'

'Enclosed,' Ross said hesitantly. 'A group of trees and bushes surround the path there, obscuring the view from Melville Drive and Fingal Place.' She shook her head. 'Only a stone's throw from the steps opposite Sylvan Place, where I live. Another few seconds and...' Her voice trailed off.

'Did you hear or see him before the assault?' Lyall asked.

Ross studied her for a long moment. 'Yes,' she said. 'Yes, come to think of it, I did. I'd just crossed the pedestrian lights at Middle Meadow Walk. A cyclist reached them before me and pressed the button. When the light changed to green he cycled off. I was aware of someone crossing behind me as I veered left towards the path, and glanced behind. I saw a man, talking into his phone.'

'Did he appear to be following you?' Mason asked.

'I didn't think so. I assumed he was heading for Argyle Place, the road opposite Middle Meadow Walk. I looked ahead and continued walking.'

'You didn't hear anything behind you?' Lyall asked.

'No. Not until…' Again she let her reply hang.

'What did he look like, the man on the phone?' Mason said.

Ross shrugged. 'I dunno, average. Medium height – five-seven or eight.'

'Did you see his face?' Lyall asked.

'Not really. It was dark. And he had the mobile clasped to his mouth.'

'What happened then?'

'On the path?'

'Yes,' Lyall replied.

'He grabbed me from behind, his hand covering my mouth. Next, I felt something cold at my neck. He said, "I've a knife at your throat, the blade pressed against your carotid artery. Create a scene or make a sound and it'll take only a moment to sever it. Nod if you understand."' Ross's lip quivered, and she continued, 'I did as he asked. A second later I was dragged into the bushes and pushed to the ground, where he forced himself on me… it must've been minutes but it seemed like an hour.'

'The man's voice,' Mason said. 'It sounded like the guy with the phone?'

'I think so,' Ross said. 'A bit hoarser, though.'

'When he…' Lyall paused, trying to frame the question in the most sensitive manner. 'When he lay over you, he was wearing the balaclava?'

'Yes.'

'You never at any point glimpsed his face or saw the clothes he was wearing?'

'No. His hand was on my mouth, my head to the ground. All I was aware of was his mask.'

'Did you see the knife?' Mason asked.

'Briefly, yes,' Ross said. 'When he pushed me down.'

'Can you describe what it looked like?'

'I only saw the blade. Thin in width, half the length of a bread knife.'

'A stiletto?'

'Could be. I saw it again briefly when he'd…' Ross took out a hankie and dabbed her eyes. 'When he'd finished. He put it to my throat a second time and told me to face the ground. Not to move till he'd gone. Told me if I didn't, he'd come back and get me. He said he knew where I lived.'

'You did as he asked?' Lyall said.

'Uh-huh. Waited a couple of minutes. When I got up, he'd gone.'

'Jan,' Mason said, 'I'm guessing the man followed you through the Meadows, but it's possible you crossed paths earlier. I'm thinking of the place where you work as a waitress. The pizza restaurant?'

'Mario's?'

'Yes. I take it you work shifts there?'

'Yes, the restaurant's open from 9am to 9pm. I work two shifts. 9am till 5pm and 1pm until 9pm, alternate weeks.'

'And this week you finish at nine?'

'Yes.'

'How many waitresses does Mario's employ?'

'On the back shift, you mean?'

'Yes.'

'Only two at the moment. Now that the Festival's over we're a bit quieter. At present it's myself and another waitress, Ellen.'

'Uh-huh,' Mason said. 'And do you recall serving any men who were there on their own last night, say between seven and eight-thirty?'

Ross's eyes flicked to the ceiling and she thought for a moment. 'Only two. One guy who came in just before eight, the other around quarter past. Tell the truth, there were only two other customers around that time, an older couple who Ellen served. Like I say, we were quiet.'

'The men,' Lyall said. 'What did they look like?'

'Both in their twenties. The first smartly dressed, dark hair. Wore a tie. Had on a navy-blue car coat, I think. The other was older, nearer thirty. Looked like a tourist. Casually dressed, carrying a backpack.'

'You served them both?'

'Yes.'

'When you took the first guy's order,' Mason said, 'were there any other customers in at the time?'

Ross shook her head. 'No, the couple came in about ten past eight. The backpacker five minutes later.'

'What was he like, the guy with the tie?'

Ross gave Mason a questioning look. 'I'm not sure what you mean.'

'What did he look like?'

'Average, I think. Nothing particular that caught my attention.'

'Did he say anything, engage you in conversation?'

'No, he said very little. Just gave me his order and thanked me when I took it to the table. His head was in a paper when I gave him his bill. He left cash on the table and left soon afterward.'

'And when you served him, the middle-aged couple hadn't arrived?'

'No, the restaurant was empty. Only Ellen and I passing the time, talking.'

'Do you recall what you were talking about?'

Ross shrugged. 'I dunno. The weather. Buses.'

'Buses?' Mason said.

'Uh-huh. Ellen was talking about the 42 service. She stays at Peffermill and told me it stops at George IV Bridge at eight minutes past nine. She complained if she doesn't get away on time she misses it, has to wait twenty minutes for the next one.'

'Did you say anything about how *you* got home, or what time you finished?'

'Uh-huh, I told her I walked home via the Meadows and she said I'd be safer taking the bus.'

Ross's face crumpled and she threw a hand to her mouth. 'Oh, my God. It was him, wasn't it? He overheard me tell Ellen where I lived, how I got home. He must've hung about and followed me.'

Mason reached over and squeezed Ross's hand. 'It's possible, Jan. Now, this is important: try to remember what time he left.'

'I can tell you exactly,' Ross said. 'Twenty-five past eight. I know that because when he went, he left a five-pound tip. I told Ellen and she joked she'd make a note of it. She said, "Gratuity of the week award goes to Jan. 8.25pm, Monday 9 September."' Ross winced. 'Bastard. I'll make sure it goes in a charity box now.'

'You've been very brave, Jan,' Lyall said. 'And very helpful. I'm sure the information you've given us will prove useful.'

'I can leave now?'

'Yes,' Lyall said. 'I'll ask Jennifer, the sergeant who brought the coffee, to give you a lift home.' Lyall paused. 'Oh, by the way, the doctor gave you an information booklet?'

The young woman took a brochure from the seat alongside her. 'Yes,' she said. 'I have it here.'

Lyall reached over and gave Ross her card. 'It's more than a hundred pages long, but take time to read it. It explains about all the help you can get – both physical and psychological. Also, on page 20, you'll find details about an emergency contraceptive pill. Take one within three days if you're worried about pregnancy. Meantime, give us a ring if you've any other concerns.' She smiled, adding, 'And don't worry, we'll be in touch the moment we find anything on your attacker.'

* * *

'Tuffnell's not changed his address with the DVLA since his licence was last registered,' Hathaway was saying. Knox and Fulton were back in the car after their interview with Everett, and the DI had phoned his colleague for an update.

'Then he must have been in Edinburgh on holiday or on business,' Knox said.

'The latter's more likely, boss,' Hathaway said. 'I Googled him after checking with the DVLA. Seems Tuffnell was a stock trader. My search brought up an article in *The Scotsman* dating from April this year. He appeared at the High Court in Edinburgh after being taken to court by three people who lost their savings as the result of a dodgy deal.'

'Go on.'

'*The Scotsman* claims the three parties had put money in a start-up firm specialising in video games that Tuffnell had recommended. The company, NewTech Holdings, was subsequently sued under copyright law by an American firm claiming intellectual property rights on one of the games marketed by NewTech. The American firm won and NewTech went bankrupt. As I said, the three lost their investment.'

'How much of an investment?'

'Two and three-quarter million.'

Knox emitted a low whistle. 'How did they get on?'

'The investors? Lost their case, I'm afraid.'

'The article, does it give the name of Tuffnell's company?'

'Fairborough and Noble Investments, 76 Charlotte Square. Apparently, he worked with them as an associate broker. I wanted to check if he was still with them, so I gave the firm a ring. They told me Tuffnell flew up from London yesterday and was having a series of meetings with the senior partner. Today and tomorrow.'

'Did you find out the senior partner's name?'

'Yes, boss. A Sir Michael Fairborough.'

'He's there this morning?'

'His secretary told me he was, yes.'

'You didn't tell her about Tuffnell's demise?'

'No, boss. Only that we'd found his driving licence.'

'Good work, Mark. Okay, Bill and I will head over to Charlotte Square now. See what Fairborough can tell us.'

Chapter Five

The entrance to Fairborough and Noble's building at 76 Charlotte Square was sleek, modern and glass-fronted, and completely incongruous with the elegant Georgian facades elsewhere in the square. Knox parked his car immediately outside, catching the attention of a uniformed parking attendant who, spotting the police sticker on the windscreen, gave a him a disconcerted look and continued on his way.

The detectives entered a short hallway with marble-faced walls, at the end of which was a wide, teak-panelled reception desk. A middle-aged woman wearing spectacles looked up as they approached. 'Good morning, gentlemen,' she said. 'How may I help you?'

Knox took out his warrant card folder and flicked it open. 'Morning,' he said. 'I'm Detective Inspector Knox, and this is my colleague Detective Sergeant Fulton. We're here to see Sir Michael Fairborough.'

The woman adjusted her glasses and glanced at a desktop computer screen. 'I see, sir. What time's your appointment?'

'I'm sorry,' Knox said. 'Perhaps you misunderstood me. We're here on police business. We don't have an appointment.'

The woman eyed Knox for a moment. 'Oh, I see,' she said, reaching for a telephone. 'I'll ring and let him know you're here.'

She straightened in her chair a moment later and said, 'Sir Michael? Allison Dalgety, sir. There are two police officers at reception. They wish to see you.'

Knox heard a faint response from the earpiece, then she glanced at the detectives. 'Yes, sir, two. A Detective Inspector Knox and a Sergeant–' She gave Knox a questioning look.

'Fulton,' Knox said.

Dalgety repeated this, and a few seconds later covered the mouthpiece. 'Sir Michael would like to know what you want to see him about.'

'His associate broker, Mr Adrian Tuffnell.'

The receptionist relayed this information, nodded, and said, 'Very well, sir. I will, yes.'

She replaced the handset, pointed to a lift at the other side of the hallway, and addressed Knox. 'First floor, sir. Sir Michael's office faces the lift entrance.'

A few moments later the lift doors opened and they saw a short man who looked to be in his early sixties. He waved to an open door across from the lift. 'Please,' he said. 'Go inside, take a seat.'

Knox and Fulton entered the office, the centrepiece of which was a solid oak desk placed in front of a window with a view to Charlotte Square Gardens. Two large filing cabinets were positioned in front of the wall on the left, beside a table on which a computer monitor displayed the latest stock market figures.

Fairborough followed them and gestured to a couple of leather-bound chairs in front of the desk. 'Go ahead, gentlemen,' he said, 'sit yourselves down.'

Knox and Fulton did so, then Fairborough went to the opposite side and sat on an executive version of the same suite of chairs.

'Would you like coffee?' he said. 'My secretary was just about to make some.'

'Thank you, no,' Knox said. 'It's not long since we had tea.'

'I see,' Fairborough said, and tapped the phone on his desk. 'Ms Dalgety rang me earlier. Said she'd received a call from one of your officers. He told her Adrian's driving licence had been found somewhere in the High Street.' He gave the detectives a supercilious smile. 'Surely that's not why you're here?'

'In a way, sir, yes,' Knox said.

Fairborough put his elbows on the table, clasped his hands together, and leaned forward. 'Really?'

'Your receptionist told my officer that Mr Tuffnell flew up from London yesterday to have talks with a senior partner in your firm,' Knox said. 'Can you confirm that person would be you?'

'Yes,' Fairborough replied, 'Adrian works with us on a contract basis. He has contacts with clients in various parts of the UK to whom he brokers shares on our behalf. He flies up from London most weeks to place these through the company.'

'And you and he were due to have a meeting today?'

Fairborough looked at his watch. '*Are* due,' he said. 'We've an appointment at ten-thirty.' He studied Knox for a long moment. 'Why do you ask?'

'I'm sorry to have to tell you this, sir. But Mr Tuffnell's body was found in a close in the High Street at seven this morning.'

'Surely not,' Fairborough said, his face a mask of disbelief. 'You're positive it's Adrian? The driving licence was definitely with the person – not in the street?'

'Yes, it was part of the contents of a wallet found on the body.'

Fairborough shook his head. 'Adrian stays at the Travelodge Hotel in St Mary's Street. I thought he may have dropped it on the way there.' He studied the detectives for a long moment. 'You think he was murdered?'

'We've reason to believe so, sir, yes.'

Fairborough emitted a deep sigh. 'Good God,' he said.

Knox took a notebook from his jacket pocket and flicked it open. 'When was the last time you saw Mr Tuffnell, sir?' he said.

'Last Wednesday. Adrian has had pretty much the same routine over the last few months. He flies up on a Monday evening and we meet here to discuss business on Tuesdays and Wednesdays, when he takes an early evening flight back to London.'

'Did you speak to him on the phone yesterday?'

'Yes. Adrian called me to confirm he'd secured a number of trades with clients in the south during the past week. We talked about finalising these when he got into the office.'

'You never discussed anything else?'

Fairborough gave Knox a piercing look. 'I'm not sure what you mean.'

'He didn't say if he was meeting anyone in Edinburgh?'

'No. You must understand, Inspector, that my relationship with Adrian was pretty much business oriented. We've dined together the odd time, but on such occasions clients were usually present. I wasn't privy to his personal life. Where he was going or who he was seeing, that sort of thing.'

'Do you know if he was married?'

Fairborough nodded. 'He divorced a couple of years back.'

'I see,' Knox said, then added, 'by the way, sir, our preliminary inquiries highlighted a case involving Mr Tuffnell at the High Court in Edinburgh last April. Are you able to tell us anything about it?'

Fairborough shrugged. 'NewTech?' he said. 'Yes, I can. The business went through our books, but the trade was initiated by Adrian and the clients were his. NewTech was a new company operating in a relatively new industry – computer games. Their business is all a bit arcane to me, but I'll tell you what I can.

'It involved two brothers – Jason and Ross Wylie – who started the firm a mere three years ago with a game called *Lancer* – something to do with medieval knights, I'm told. Anyway, it proved a best-seller and they followed with several others, all equally successful. Then, in 2018, the Wylies came up with a new game, which I believe had something of a dystopian theme. Apparently, it was considerably more complex to engineer, so the brothers took NewTech public in order to raise funds.

'They chose Adrian to handle sales of the shares, which proved successful and within a very short period the release was oversubscribed. The game went to market and sales skyrocketed. Then, a month or so later, a giant US company discovered it to be an almost exact copy of one of their own, which had just launched in America. They sued the Wylies for a breach of intellectual copyright and won a five-million-dollar lawsuit, which of course bankrupted NewTech. Adrian knew three of the company's biggest investors personally, who between them had suffered the greatest loss – almost three million pounds. They claimed Adrian had foreknowledge of the brothers' plagiarism and sued him. The High Court found their claim unproven, however, and they lost their case.'

'Who were the three investors?' Knox said.

'If you give me a moment, I'll get them for you,' Fairborough said. 'We have their files on our system.'

At that moment there was a knock at the door and a slim woman entered carrying a tray on which was a silver coffee pot, together with cup, milk and sugar. 'Your coffee, Sir Michael,' she said.

'Thank you, Allison,' Fairborough said, then inclined his head towards Knox and Fulton. 'You're sure you won't have some, detectives?'

Knox shook his head and Fulton followed his lead. 'No, sir,' he said. 'Thank you for offering.'

The woman set down the tray on Fairborough's desk and was about to leave when her boss raised his hand, motioning her to wait. 'Oh, Allison,' he said.

'Sir?'

'The people who took Mr Tuffnell to court in April. We still have their details on file?'

'Yes, sir. We have.'

'Could you let me have a print-out with their names and addresses?'

Fairborough's secretary dipped her head in acknowledgement. 'Of course, sir,' she said, then exited the office.

* * *

'What do you think, boss?' Fulton said when he and Knox got back to the car. 'Fairborough's telling the truth?'

'About how involved he was with Tuffnell over NewTech, you mean?'

'Aye.'

Knox shrugged. 'His firm got their cut when the deal was floated, he admitted that much. And Tuffnell brought in the business.'

'No reason to make him a suspect, then? The case didn't affect him.'

'Apart from a bit of adverse publicity?' Knox said. 'It would seem not. He and Tuffnell carried on, business as usual.' Knox opened a manila envelope, took out an A4 sheet of paper, and flattened it on his lap. 'No,' he said, tapping the sheet, 'I think this might prove a better starting point. These are the folk with a real grievance.'

He scanned the paper for a few moments, then said, 'One here in Edinburgh, one down the coast in Gullane, the third in Stirling.'

'Who's the one in Edinburgh?' Fulton asked.

Knox ran his finger down the page. 'Maxwell Denison, 74 Easter Belmont Road, Corstorphine.' Knox paused. 'Hmm,' he said. 'Denison appears to have been the largest investor. One million, seven hundred and twenty-five thousand.'

'Helluva lot to kiss goodbye to,' Fulton said.

'You can say that again. I think—' Knox was interrupted by a sudden ringing. He took his mobile from his pocket, placed it on the dashboard, and switched it to the car's speakers. 'Yvonne,' he said.

'Boss,' Mason replied. 'Checking in with an update. Kate and I completed our interview with Jan Ross.'

'Anything new?' Knox asked.

'A wee bit more encouraging, yes. We discovered the attacker followed her from George IV Bridge. He was a customer at the restaurant; overheard her tell another waitress where she stayed and that she walked home. Kate and I went to George IV Bridge to look for CCTV. The General Commercial Bank branch on the corner of Chambers Street has one. Gave us access to the recording.'

'He's on tape?'

'Yes. Got a good view of him crossing George IV Bridge and following her into Forrest Road.'

'How good a view?'

'Only his back, I'm afraid. But the height matches the description Jan Ross gave us: around five-eight and dark-haired. Well-dressed. Wearing a navy-blue car coat, black trousers and shoes.'

'Well that's something, anyway – we didn't get CCTV in the other two cases?'

'No. Rachel Miller was attacked in the entrance hallway of her flat when she arrived home, Alice Cairns at the foot of the stairwell of the block where she lives. Both women stay in residential areas; no CCTV.'

'But there was a DNA match?'

'Yes,' Mason said. 'The same man raped both Alice Cairns and Rachel Miller. The only thing different in Jan Ross's case is the balaclava mask; neither Cairns nor Miller reported their attacker wearing one.'

'You think that pertinent?'

'No. Kate and I agree he probably had one with him. Just didn't need to use it with the first two rapes. We're confident when the DNA results come back from the lab at Howdenhall we'll get a match.' She paused for a moment, and added, 'We're going to re-interview both Cairns and Miller anyway, see if we've missed anything.'

Knox checked his watch. 'Okay. It's 11am now, you'll manage to squeeze in both interviews today?'

'We'll try,' Mason said. 'Alice Cairns runs a dog grooming service in Portobello. Likely we'll find her there. Rachel Miller works in an office near her place in Salamander Street in Leith. We have her mobile, though; we'll give her a ring and check when she's home.'

'Okay,' Knox said. 'Bill and I are likely to be out of the office, too, for a while.'

'I forgot to ask,' Mason said. 'The body at Netherbow, it's definitely murder?'

'No question,' Knox replied, and brought her up to date on their interviews with Everett and Fairborough.

'So you think one of the investors is likely to be the murderer?'

'Well, they all had motive, that's for sure,' Knox said. 'And the means. Only leaves us to discover which one had the opportunity.'

Chapter Six

Knox keyed in the number Fairborough's secretary had given him, which rang five times before a female voice answered.

'Good morning,' Knox said. 'May I speak to Mr Maxwell Denison, please?'

'Who's calling?'

'Detective Inspector Knox, Gayfield Square Police Station. Is Mr Denison at home?'

There was a long silence on the line, which led Knox to think he'd been cut off. 'Hello?' he said.

'I'm still here,' the woman replied. 'My father died three months ago.'

'I'm sorry to hear that,' Knox said. 'Who am I speaking to?'

'His daughter, Christine Dalrymple, née Denison.'

'I see,' Knox said. 'May I speak to Mrs Denison, then?'

'My mother's in a care home,' the woman replied. 'Why are you calling?'

'It's in connection with Mr Denison's investment with a company called NewTech,' Knox replied. 'We're investigating the death of the man who sold shares to your father, a Mr Adrian Tuffnell.'

'Tuffnell's dead?'

'I'm sorry to have tell you so, yes.'

Knox heard a snort on the line. 'Well, I'm not sorry to have to hear it.'

'Really?' Knox said. 'May I ask why?'

'Tuffnell conned my father into investing his life savings to promote a project he knew to be dubious. It broke my father; caused him to take his own life.'

'You knew about the deal?'

'Yes, Tuffnell was a charlatan. I tried to dissuade my father from going ahead with it.'

Knox glanced at his watch. 'Mrs Dalrymple,' he said. 'We've good reason to believe Mr Tuffnell was murdered. I'd like to find out more about his dealings with your father. Would it be possible to come and talk to you?'

'Today?'

'Yes. Within the next hour, if you're free.'

'It won't take long? I've a dental appointment at two-thirty.'

'Around half an hour, I should think.'

'Okay.'

'Thank you, Mrs Dalrymple,' Knox replied. 'Be with you shortly.'

* * *

Easter Belmont Road was accessed via an inconspicuous entrance at the top end of Murrayfield Road in the city's western suburbs. Knox drove along the narrow cul-de-sac, where a series of substantial-looking villas lined the roadway at either side. He drove almost to the end, then the computerised voice of his sat nav announced, 'Seventy-four Easter Belmont Road. You have reached your destination.'

Knox stopped, applied the handbrake and put the gear lever in neutral, wound down the window and surveyed the property. The house, girdled by a low wall, sat at the top of an incline approached by a tarmac driveway that meandered down a wide, sloping lawn.

'Not for nothing this place is known as Millionaires' Row, boss,' Fulton said. 'I hear properties in the street sell for upwards of two million.'

'Doesn't surprise me,' Knox said, his attention taken by a small, square grill-fronted box affixed to the gate.

Suddenly a tinny-sounding voice come from a speaker at the other side of the grill: 'You're Inspector Knox – the policeman I spoke to on the phone?'

'Yes. Mrs Dalrymple?'

'Ah-huh. Wait a moment and I'll open the gates, they're electronically controlled. The entrance to the house is at the end of the driveway.'

As the gates swung open, Knox put his car into gear and continued up the driveway, coming to a halt at a portico at the side of the house. He and Fulton exited and were met by a slim woman Knox took to be in her mid-thirties. She motioned to the door with a wave of her hand. 'Please, go through to the lounge, it's at the end of the hallway on your right.'

The detectives did as she asked and found themselves in a large room where the floral-patterned curtains at the windows matched the covers of the sofa and chairs.

Dalrymple came in behind them, closed the door, and pointed to the sofa. 'Please,' she said. 'Sit yourselves down.'

When they complied, she added, 'You found me, okay, then? People new to the area sometimes tell me they've a devil of a job locating the entrance at Murrayfield Road.'

Knox smiled and thumbed upwards. 'With a little bit of help.'

'Ah, yes,' Dalrymple said. 'Sat nav. Where would we be without it?'

'Lost?' Fulton volunteered, grinning.

Dalrymple gave a little laugh. 'Yes,' she agreed. 'Quite.' She took a seat opposite and addressed Knox. 'Okay,' she said, 'to the point of your visit. You wanted to ask about Tuffnell's association with my father?'

'Yes,' Knox said. 'I was wondering how he came to be involved with Adrian Tuffnell?'

'They met two years ago,' Dalrymple said. 'Shortly before Fraser Noble – Sir Michael Fairborough's partner in the investment firm – died after a short battle with cancer. You see, my father had gone to Fettes College with Fraser and they were close friends. When Fraser started up the firm with Fairborough back in the eighties my father was one of the first investors. Over the years it proved a profitable relationship. Fraser had a good eye for the markets, and helped make my father's fortunes. However, when Fraser's ill-health forced him to retire from the business, Sir Michael brought in Tuffnell to handle his clients, which was when he took charge of my father's portfolio.'

Dalrymple took a packet of Rothmans and a lighter from an occasional table next to her armchair and extracted a cigarette. 'You mind if I smoke?'

'No,' Knox said. 'Carry on.'

Dalrymple flicked the lighter, drew on the cigarette, and exhaled. 'Tuffnell impressed my father in the beginning by recommending a couple of internet-based companies which proved to be good investments. So by the time NewTech came along he trusted Tuffnell's instincts.'

'But one and three-quarter million pounds is a significant amount of money,' Knox said. 'He didn't have reservations?'

Dalrymple shook her head. 'That's the pity of it. My father was distracted, under great strain. My mother's been suffering from Alzheimer's for some time. In the past three years, however, she deteriorated considerably. I told you she's in a care home?'

'You mentioned it, yes,' Knox said.

Dalrymple shook her head. 'Well, my brother and I decided it would be easier on my father if she received round-the-clock attention. In the early part of last year we persuaded him it would in their best interests if she was taken into care.'

She tapped her cigarette on an ashtray and went on, 'My father was worried about the long-term costs of looking after her. My brother and I tried to assure him his finances were secure, but he fretted about it to the point of obsession. He thought he could bolster them with the NewTech deal, which Tuffnell persuaded him was a sure thing.'

'But you had your doubts?'

'Yes. Just a feeling at first. Based on nothing other than instant dislike of the man the first time I met him.'

'Where was that?'

'At Fraser Noble's funeral, when my father introduced him to Edward and me.'

'Edward?' Knox said.

'My brother.'

'I see.'

'My father liked him, of course. And, more importantly, trusted him. Particularly after the first two investments with the internet companies bore fruit.' Dalrymple drew on her cigarette again, exhaled, and continued, 'I didn't see Tuffnell much after Fraser's funeral, and first heard about the NewTech investment when Edward phoned me in July last year.

'He and his wife Jennifer and their daughter Hannah were visiting Father one Saturday afternoon when the phone rang. Hannah was in the garden playing with her grandfather and Edward took the call. It was from Sir Michael. He told Edward the NewTech contract was ready for signing and would my father bring in the cheque the following Monday. He asked Edward to pass on the message.

'Edward was in the dark, of course. He asked Fairborough to explain, and Sir Michael told him about NewTech and my father's investment. Edward was curious. He asked Sir Michael about the amount, and was taken aback when Fairborough told him. Naturally, my brother was concerned. He rang me, and I drove over that evening and we sat with Father and discussed it. One and three-quarter million pounds represented almost all of his capital. My brother and I knew he'd been under a lot of stress with my mother and were worried he might be acting under duress. We questioned the wisdom of putting all his financial eggs in one basket. He refused to listen, however, saying he had every confidence in Tuffnell's judgement.'

'You said you believed Tuffnell knew the deal to be flawed,' Knox said. 'That he had foreknowledge of the NewTech copyright breach?'

Dalrymple nodded. 'I told you I didn't like Tuffnell,' she replied. 'Neither did Edward. My brother met him a week after Father signed the deal. He'd visited Fairborough to seek more information on NewTech. Sir Michael claimed he knew little about it, emphasising it was Tuffnell's project. My brother spoke to Tuffnell, who assured him NewTech's game – the one our father had invested so heavily in – was unique. He was confident it would prove a success.'

Dalrymple stubbed her cigarette in the ashtray. 'Edward wasn't convinced. He sought the advice of a friend in Dundee, where the gaming industry is based. The man made inquiries and discovered that a year earlier the Wylies had marketed a game which turned out to be the intellectual property of a company called ADL studios.'

'The Wylies were sued?' Knox asked.

'No, it was settled out of court. Apparently NewTech apologised and immediately withdrew the game, and the company were satisfied.

'Edward now had real doubts and asked his friend to dig deeper. The man discovered NewTech's new game was called *Armageddon 2*, and it was common knowledge in the industry that some scenes had been lifted directly from *Generation 2042*, a game just released in America.

'Edward telephoned Tuffnell, and he informed my brother that the Wylies knew about the American game. He told Edward he'd personally viewed both *Armageddon 2* and *Generation 2042* and promised him the NewTech game was completely new. However, a month later NewTech received a writ from the American firm's lawyers and was taken to court, where theft of intellectual copyright was proven. The subsequent five-million-dollar lawsuit bankrupted NewTech.'

'Your father sued Tuffnell in turn?' Knox said.

'Yes, together with two other investors. Tuffnell had claimed *Armageddon 2* was original. He stated in court this wasn't true: he had made no such statement to my brother. He insisted he'd been taken in by the Wylies as much as my father had. My brother was unable to prove the conversation had taken place, of course, and we lost the case.'

'This was last April?'

'Yes,' Dalrymple said. 'The outcome broke my father. The financial loss coincided with a marked change in my mother. Until then she'd greeted him with a smile each time he visited her; suddenly she failed to recognise him. Father lost his appetite, not only for food, but for life. Even Hannah, whose visits he normally looked forward to, failed to change his mood. Then one Sunday afternoon last June Edward found him in the garage. He'd committed suicide with a shotgun he used for grouse shooting.'

'Your brother lives in Edinburgh?' Knox asked.

'Yes,' Dalrymple replied. 'In Colinton Avenue. Only a couple of streets from where I stay.' She waved to her surroundings. 'You caught me here today because I was sorting out some of Father's things. My brother and I will be putting this house on the market soon.'

She reached into her handbag and took out a card, which she gave Knox. 'My home and mobile telephone numbers,' she said, 'in case you want to speak to me again.'

Knox took the card, then closed his notebook and put both in his jacket pocket. 'Thank you, Mrs Dalrymple,' he said. 'You've been very helpful.'

Chapter Seven

It had been the lead story on local radio that morning, and he'd spotted sensationalist headlines on billboards outside newspaper shops as he drove to his destination: "Masked Rapist Claims Third Victim".

Most young women would be on their guard now, he reasoned, which meant it was less likely he'd come across targets of opportunity, as Jan the waitress and the other women had been.

No, he'd have to change tack. He'd been wary of taking advantage of his job to find new conquests, but unless he was prepared to lie low for an indeterminate amount of time, he could see no alternative.

It wasn't the first time he'd given it serious thought. As a rep for a leading letting agent he met dozens of women every week, a situation he was uniquely placed to take advantage of. It came with a great deal of risk, of course. If he wasn't exceptionally careful, he'd be the first on the cop's radar.

But if he did his homework and planned for every eventuality, he should get away with it. He'd have to prepare meticulously, and in every case make sure there was a strong possibility an assailant had other means of accessing the victim.

He flicked the indicator, turned left from Bruntsfield Place into Viewforth, and gave a little smile. He'd been sent to check out a flat at Viewforth Square which had just been made available for rent. A couple of Polish girls were interested in taking a six-month lease, his boss informed him. He had to make sure everything was in order first, then take the women up for a viewing tomorrow.

The girls had been leaving the office as he entered, and they'd exchanged smiles. One of them, an attractive blonde, held eye contact for a long moment as they passed each other. He felt a stirring in his groin now, just thinking of her. He slowed his car on approach to Viewforth Square and smiled again. If he was careful in laying the groundwork, she might prove his ideal next conquest.

* * *

Portobello Pet Parlour was situated at 390 High Street, Portobello, a seaside town on Edinburgh's eastern periphery. Lyall parked her Vectra outside the premises and she and Mason exited and walked to the entrance.

Alice Cairns had shoulder-length strawberry-blonde hair and was seated behind a desk near the door. She looked up in surprise as they came inside. 'You've arrested him?' she said.

Lyall shook her head. 'Sorry, Alice, we haven't. But there's been a bit of a development. We'd like to go over a couple of things with you.' She nodded to the rear of the shop. 'If you're not busy, that is.'

Cairns glanced at her watch. 'No. My next appointment isn't till eleven-thirty, another half hour.' She pointed to an upholstered bench positioned at right-angles to the desk. 'You'd better take a seat.' A pause, then, 'This is to do with the girl who was raped in the Meadows last night, isn't it?'

Mason nodded. 'Yes,' she said. 'There are similarities.'

The detectives sat and Lyall reached into a leather satchel and took out an A4-sized folder. 'We've brought your case notes, Alice,' she said. 'We'd like to go over your statement again in case there's anything we've missed. Is that okay?'

Cairns nodded. 'Uh-huh,' she said quietly.

'I know the assault is still very much on your mind, Alice,' Lyall said sympathetically, 'and that revisiting it might be painful, but I assure you we wouldn't ask if we didn't think it necessary.'

Cairns bit her lip. 'I understand.'

'Okay,' Lyall said. 'Let's start at the beginning. You were assaulted near the back door of your block of flats at 17 Mayburn Terrace, Joppa, at approximately 8.30pm on Wednesday 14 August, is that correct?'

'Yes,' Cairns replied. 'I'd locked up the shop around six-thirty and drove to Asda at Brunstane. I do a weekly shop and had a full trolley load – eight or nine carrier bags. I brought them into the stair – I had to make two trips. I left the first lot in the stairwell while I brought in the remainder. I'm on the second floor, so I leave the bags in the stairwell, take some to my flat, and come back for the others.

'Anyway, it was my last trip down. I was about to lift the remaining bags when I heard a scuffle behind me. I made to turn but didn't get a chance. He came at me from behind. Grabbed my hair and pushed me to the back door.'

'There was no one near when you took your shopping from the car?' Mason asked.

'No,' Cairns said. 'I parked where I normally do – the residents' car park alongside the flats. It was still quite light. If there had been someone there, I'm sure I'd have spotted him.'

'Could someone have followed you home from the supermarket?' Lyall asked.

Cairns shook her head. 'No, I've thought about that since the first time you interviewed me. As I told you then, I didn't pay much attention. But I'm sure no other car stopped when I parked.'

'The stair door,' Mason said. 'It doesn't have a key?'

'No – well, yes, actually. It has one of those old-style locks with a large opening that looks like an upside-down T. You're supposed to insert a key that lifts a drop bar on the inside. Though anyone can manipulate it by inserting a pinkie and pushing up. The key's in the flat somewhere, but I've never used it.'

Lyall glanced at the folder. 'You told us he forced you along the passage towards the back door?'

'Yes, a short corridor leading to the back gardens.' Cairns shuddered visibly. 'He had a knife at my throat. I couldn't see it but felt it, against my neck.'

'The overhead light wasn't working?' Mason said.

'No, the bulb needed replacing.'

'What happened next?' Lyall said.

'I was forced down and turned onto my back – which was when I was aware of the knife. He had my head pressed to the ground.'

'He said anything?' Mason asked.

'Yes. Something about the blade of the knife being pressed against an artery.'

'The carotid artery?'

'That's right. Said it would only take a minute to slit my throat if I made a sound.'

'You never saw his face at any point,' Lyall said, 'not even a glimpse?'

Cairns shook her head. 'No. It was almost totally dark. When it was...' She paused, swallowing. 'When it was over he made me lie face down. I was terrified. I remember feeling the knife at my neck again. I was convinced he was going to stab me. He said, "I'm leaving now, but if you move or say anything, I'll come back and kill you."'

'Then he left?' Mason said.

'Yes,' Cairns replied. 'I lay for a while after I heard the stair door close, just to be sure. Like I said, I was terrified.'

'I know you couldn't see him,' Lyall said, 'but do you think he was wearing a mask?'

Cairns thought for a moment. 'You know, come to think of it, he could have been. He only spoke twice, but at one point his voice sounded a bit muffled.'

'As if he was speaking through some sort of face covering?' Mason said.

'Yes,' Cairns said. She looked Mason directly in the eye. 'The guy responsible for the Meadows rape, he wore a mask too. Didn't he?'

'Yes, Alice,' Mason replied. 'He did.'

* * *

'What do you think, boss?' Fulton was saying. 'Dalrymple and her brother both have a strong motive for wanting Tuffnell dead.'

The detectives were back in the car and Knox had stopped at a set of pedestrian lights in Roseburn Terrace, part of the western approach to Edinburgh city centre.

'A very strong motive,' Knox agreed. He took out the sheet Fairborough's secretary had printed and glanced at it. 'But then so do the two other investors.' He replaced the paper in the glovebox as the lights changed to green. 'Mr Reginald Coutts in Gullane and a Miss Frances Mainwaring in Stirling.'

'You're going to see the Gullane investor first?'

Knox glanced at his watch. 'Almost half twelve now,' he said. 'I'll give him a ring, see if he'll see us after lunch. I'm going to find out if Turley has the results of the PM first.'

Knox highlighted the pathologist's number on his telephone mounted on the dash and pressed *call*. The ring tone sounded through the car's speakers, then a woman's voice answered: 'Hello, Cowgate Mortuary.'

'Maisie? DI Knox. Could I speak to Mr Turley, please?'

'Afternoon, Inspector,' the receptionist replied. 'Hang on, I'll see if I can get him for you.'

There was a short silence, then Knox heard Turley say, 'Jack?'

'Afternoon, Alex. You've completed the PM on Adrian Tuffnell?'

'Aye, a short while ago.' Knox heard the rustle of paper, and Turley continued, 'A thorough examination confirmed my initial findings: intracerebral hematoma caused by repeated blows to the head. Death followed due to blood loss over a period of two or three hours.'

'You told me this morning you suspected an attempt at strangulation?'

'Aye, Jack. I was coming to that. As I told you earlier, contusions indicate some constriction of the larynx. Looking at the affected area in more detail, I observed a two-centimetre-wide line around the thyroid cartilage – the Adam's apple – indicative of a thin cord or similar being drawn around the neck.'

'This would have been looped from behind?'

'I think so, going by the degree of pressure. It's also extremely likely he was dragged a short distance.'

'Thanks, Alex,' Knox said. 'That's helpful.'

'One other thing, Jack. Tuffnell had been drinking. He had a blood alcohol level of 0.08 – equivalent to four or five whiskies or four pints of beer.'

'So, a bit unsteady on his feet?'

'I'd say so,' Truly replied, and added, 'Murray and Beattie haven't been in touch yet about the results of the DNA tests?'

'No,' Knox replied. 'More than likely that'll come back from the Howdenhall lab this afternoon.'

'I see,' Turley said. 'Okay, Jack. Speak to you later.'

'Right, Alex. Again, many thanks.'

Knox ended the call and turned to Fulton. 'Well, that rules out one possibility,' he said. 'That Christine

Dalrymple acted on her own. Tuffnell was too big and heavy a bloke.'

'But together with her brother?'

'Possible,' Knox said. He pulled into the kerb near Shandwick Place, a short distance from Princes Street and keyed a number into the phone. Again ringing reverberated through the speakers.

Moments later a male voice answered. An autocratic, gravelly timbre. 'Brigadier Coutts.'

'Mr Reginald Coutts?' Knox asked.

'Yes,' the man replied haughtily. 'Ex-army. Still in the reserves. I prefer to be addressed by my military rank.' A pause, then, 'Who's speaking?'

'Detective Inspector Knox, sir, based at Gayfield Square. We're investigating the death of a Mr Adrian Tuffnell in Edinburgh this morning. I was wondering if it would be possible to come down and speak to you?'

'Tuffnell was murdered?'

'Looks that way, sir, yes.'

The detectives heard him clear his throat. 'Why do you want to speak to me?'

'We believe you've had dealings with Mr Tuffnell, sir. You had shares in NewTech, a company he recommended. It was declared bankrupt?'

'Yes.'

'And, together with other investors, you took Mr Tuffnell to court?'

'Yes,' Coutts replied. 'And with good reason. Tuffnell encouraged us to purchase shares in the full knowledge that NewTech was in breach of intellectual copyright.'

'Yes, Mrs Christine Dalrymple, Mr Denison's daughter, did explain that. But I'd still like to speak to you.'

'Our grievance with Tuffnell automatically makes us suspects, is that it?'

'Not necessarily, sir. We're obliged to carry out procedure.'

Coutts harrumphed. 'Oh, very well. You want to come down this afternoon?'

'If it's convenient, sir, yes.'

'Right. But make it after two-thirty, will you? I'm about to have lunch.'

Chapter Eight

The flat was on the second floor. He let himself in with the key they'd given him at the office, walked along a narrow hallway, and entered the living room. It was rear-facing and sparsely furnished: a coffee table, sofa and armchairs occupied the centre, with a teak-veneered sideboard and a bookcase positioned opposite. At the far wall an ornamental mantelpiece framed the fireplace, in front of which sat a small electric fire.

He went to one of the two windows and looked outside, then gave a gasp of surprise. 'Is that what I think it is?' he muttered.

He exited the living room, went to the adjoining bedroom, and crossed to the window. *Yes, it is– a fire escape!* What's more, the section of steps from the flats above ended at a platform just outside, then descended to the back court via a similar platform at the flat below.

He exited the bedroom and checked out the remainder of the flat. Across the hallway was a second bedroom. Front-facing, smaller. Next to this a bathroom and kitchen, also front-facing.

He went back to the larger bedroom and took a closer look. The frame of the window was original; apparently unchanged from when the flats were built. The rail where the lower and upper sash met was secured by an old-fashioned swivelling lock. He turned it to the open position, pulled at the bottom sash, and the window slid up without effort. He closed it, jiggled the catch between his thumb and forefinger, and found there was a significant amount of play. He took a penknife from his pocket, slid the blade through the gap between lower and upper sash, and pressed against the metal. The catch swung open.

Brilliant! He would make a copy of the back door key, and climb to the bedroom via the fire escape. Then it was just a matter of inserting the blade, opening the catch, and drawing up the bottom sash. *A piece of cake.* Now all he had to do was make sure it was the blonde who took the back bedroom…

* * *

Thirty-six Ballencrieff Links was located at the far end of Gullane on the road to North Berwick. The two-storey villa was screened by a row of trees and accessed via a circular gravel driveway, which lead to an imposing-looking entrance flanked by a pair of Corinthian columns.

The detectives exited the car and went to the door, where Knox thumbed a ceramic bell-push inset into a large brass panel. A moment later the door was opened by a tall, elderly man who wore a white jacket and white shirt with black bow tie.

He gave the detectives a lugubrious look. 'Yes?'

'Detective Inspector Knox and Detective Sergeant Fulton,' Knox said. 'We're here to see Brigadier Coutts.'

'He's expecting you?'

'Yes,' Knox replied. 'We telephoned earlier.'

The man shook his head. 'He didn't tell me.' A pause, then, 'One moment please.'

Knox and Fulton exchanged glances, and moments later the man returned. 'He's in the drawing room,' he said curtly. 'Follow me.'

The man led them along a wood-panelled corridor to a front-facing room near the end. He knocked the door, opened it, and announced, 'The detectives, Brigadier.'

Knox heard Coutts say, 'Show them in, Turner, there's a good chap.'

The man opened the door and waved them inside, then departed. The detectives entered and saw Coutts seated on a leather armchair alongside a small rosewood table, on which sat a whisky decanter and glasses.

Coutts pointed to a chaise longue opposite, which Knox took to be Regency, as it was of a similar vintage to other furniture in the room. 'Take the weight off, eh, men?' he said. Then, indicating the decanter, he added, 'I was just about to have a snifter. Talisker. You'll take a glass?'

Knox shook his head. 'We appreciate your offer, sir, but no thanks.'

'Of course,' Coutts said. 'I forgot. You're on duty.'

As the detective took a seat Knox gave Coutts a quick appraisal. He was in his late fifties or early sixties. Medium height, five foot eight or nine. A little thick through the waist. Not fat, but probably nowhere near as lean as he'd been in his military days. A good head of hair, greying at the sides. He was clean-shaven and his cheeks, florid and red-veined, bore testimony to his liking for whisky.

'You'll have to excuse Turner,' he continued. 'My manservant. A trifle eccentric and a wee bit cantankerous. He was my father's batman, though, so he's something of a family retainer. He was annoyed, I forgot to tell him you were coming.'

Knox nodded. 'That's okay, sir,' he said. 'We understand.'

Coutts took the decanter and filled one of the glasses to the brim. 'Okay,' he said. 'To the subject of your visit:

Tuffnell. Christine told you her brother Edward discovered his duplicity?'

'She told us that her brother had a friend based in Dundee who had knowledge of the business, sir, yes.'

Coutts took a swig of whisky, returned the glass to the table, and nodded. 'His Dundonian friend's name is Arthur Lawson; he and Edward were schoolmates at George Heriot's. Lawson has a part-share in TayImage, one of the companies producing the games. It doesn't take long until anything new gets onto the grapevine – it's that sort of business. You're aware Lawson told Edward about the Wylies' attempt to copy a game from a company called ADL studios?'

'Yes,' Knox replied.

'Apparently NewTech got away with the skin of their teeth on that one. One of the directors of ADL knew the Wylies, which is why they agreed to settle out of court.'

'I see,' Knox said. 'And sometime after Mr Denison Senior bought shares in NewTech, his son discovered their game had similarities with the newly-released American one?'

'More than a few, Inspector. Lawson found they'd copied almost thirty per cent.'

'Edward Denison was concerned. He contacted Tuffnell?'

'Indeed he did. Tuffnell said he'd seen both, and that the NewTech game bore no resemblance. Edward voiced his concerns to Christine, who contacted me and Mrs Mainwaring. But by then it was too late. The copyright breach had been picked up by ETL International, the American company. They took NewTech to the cleaners. The Wylies declared bankruptcy after the lawsuit, and we lost our investment. We took Tuffnell to court, of course, but he swore blind the conversation between himself and Edward hadn't taken place. His brief pleaded hearsay, and he was right: we'd absolutely no proof. It was the outcome I expected, to be honest.

'Mr Denison suffered the most. He'd obviously been under tremendous strain with his wife, but Christine told me it was the depletion of his capital that drove him to suicide.'

'Did you see Mr Tuffnell after the court case?'

'No,' Coutts said adamantly. 'I've had absolutely no dealings with the bugger since. Neither he nor Fairborough. I transferred my business immediately after the court case.' Coutts downed the remaining whisky and extended a finger towards Knox. 'Look, Inspector,' he continued, 'I know I have reason to wish the man dead, as have the others, but I assure you the last time I saw Tuffnell was on April 12, in court.'

'Then you won't mind telling me where you were last night, sir,' Knox said. 'Late evening. You understand why I ask?'

Coutts refilled his glass and Knox saw his hands shake a little. 'Of course,' he replied, and nodded to the window. 'I played a round of golf at my local club, Muirfield. Perhaps you saw the clubhouse as you drove in? I finished the game around eight-thirty, and afterwards wound up at the nineteenth hole. From nine until eleven. The stewards should be only too happy to verify if you ask. I'm a very good tipper, you see.'

* * *

'I start back next Monday,' Rachel Miller was saying. 'My boss was very understanding. She gave me three weeks paid leave and insisted I return only when I felt able.' The young woman was seated in the living room of her flat in Salamander Street together with Lyall and Mason, and the detectives had phoned and arranged to meet after lunch.

'You're feeling better?' Mason said. 'Your doctor was treating you for depression?'

'I am now,' Miller said. 'I had to stop taking the tablets he prescribed, though, they were making me woozy. But soon afterwards I joined a therapy group for women who've suffered abuse. I've found talking to others helps.'

'I told you on the phone we wanted to speak about the assault, Rachel,' Lyall said. 'You're sure you're okay with it?'

Miller leaned forwards and clasped her hands together. 'I think so.'

Lyall unzipped her folder and took out a file and opened it. 'Okay,' she said. 'The twenty-ninth of August. You arrived here at approximately 5.30pm?'

Miller nodded. 'Yes, I'm only a ten-minute walk from the office in Baltic Street. I finish at five, and stopped off at a shop on the way back to get a few things. Uh-huh, it would've been around five-thirty.'

'We noticed the stair is accessed with a key,' Mason said. 'And you buzzed us in today after we pressed the intercom. Do you remember if that door was closed after you entered on August 29?'

Miller thought for a moment. 'Yes, I'm almost sure it was.'

'You saw no one in the stair?' Lyall asked.

'No. I passed a neighbour on my way back from the shops, Mrs Cuthbert, and said hello, but nobody else.'

'Mrs Cuthbert stays in one of the flats?' Mason asked.

'Yes, 437/5, the floor above me.'

'You heard no one, either?' Lyall said.

'Not then, no,' Miller said. 'I turned the key in the lock, put the carrier bag in the hall, and was reaching for the light switch when I heard scuffling. I made to turn, and that's when he pounced.'

Lyall glanced at her notes. 'Just to confirm, Rachel. You told us you didn't get a look at his face?'

'No. As I told you at the time, he grabbed my hair and forced my head first onto the floor. I think he must have used his heel to close the door, cutting off any light from the stair. Only then did he turn me onto my back. It was almost completely dark, I saw nothing.'

Lyall checked the folder again. 'Which was when you felt the knife at your throat?'

Miller clasped her hands tighter, her knuckles whitening. 'Yes,' she said. 'He threatened to cut my throat if I didn't do as he asked.' She nodded to a television in the corner of the room, which was tuned to an online shopping channel. 'They reported another assault on the Scottish news at one-thirty. In the Meadows. It's the same man, isn't it?'

Mason dipped her head in acknowledgement. 'We think it might be, yes.'

Lyall closed the folder. 'We know you were unable to see him, Rachel. He forced you to face the floor after the assault, then made his exit. The man who carried out the Meadows attack wore a balaclava mask. Did you get any sense that your attacker might have been wearing one?'

'No, I don't think so.' She paused. 'There was one thing, though, which I've remembered since I last spoke to you.'

'Oh?' Lyall said. 'What was that?'

'A strong smell of aftershave. It lingered in the hallway for a long time after he'd gone.'

Chapter Nine

'Two investigations, both of equal importance,' Knox said, then turned to the other detectives, who were seated at their desks in the Major Incident Inquiry Room at Gayfield Square Police Station.

He stood beside a large whiteboard, on which he'd detailed both cases, separated by a dividing line. 'Although we're effectively two teams,' he continued, 'we'll pool our resources. Kate and Yvonne's primary concern is the rapes, while Bill, Mark and myself will concentrate on the World's End murder. But I want you all to familiarise yourselves with, and help to solve, both cases.'

He tapped the marker on the left side of the board. 'Okay, the murder first: Mr Adrian Tuffnell, aged sixty-three, a contract broker with Fairborough and Noble in Charlotte Square. Found bludgeoned to death in World's End Close at 7am this morning by local resident, James Everett. The pathologist informs us cause of death was prolonged bleeding as a result of a severe head wound.

'Mr Tuffnell had been taken to court by three clients, each of whom lost a substantial amount of money.' He tapped the board. 'Here are the names, together with approximate losses. Christine Dalrymple and Brigadier

Coutts we've already spoken to, Mrs Mainwaring we'll interview in the morning. I hope to arrange an interview with Edward Denison later. Any questions?'

'Yes, boss,' Lyall said. 'You've not established where Christine Dalrymple was last night. I was wondering why?'

'Good question, Kate,' Knox said. 'I'll do so after I see her brother. He discovered NewTech's dishonesty and initiated the court case against Tuffnell. I'd like to speak to him first.'

'But surely they had the greatest incentive?' Mason said. 'Their father's suicide, loss of their inheritance?'

'Can't argue with that, Yvonne.'

Fulton turned to Knox. 'Coutts wasn't that convincing, either,' he said. 'I told you afterwards that I thought he might be hiding something.'

'I know,' Knox said. 'We'll check his alibi, Bill, don't worry.'

'Tuffnell was staying at the Travelodge Hotel in St Mary's Street,' Mason said. 'Did he frequent any local restaurants or pubs?'

Fulton shrugged. 'Possible, Yvonne. Maybe he was doing a bit of socialising.'

'Which begs the question,' Lyall said. 'Who was he with?'

'I'd thought about that,' Hathaway said. 'And wondered about CCTV. So I checked if there was any near the locus. There're two: both located at a clothes shop at the corner of St Mary's Street and the Canongate.'

'Good work, Mark,' Knox said. 'You can follow that up later.'

Knox indicated the right-hand side of the whiteboard. 'Right – the rapes. We'll start with Jan Ross, the latest victim.' He glanced at the women and continued, 'Yvonne, you said this morning her attacker wore a face mask, something that hadn't been mentioned?'

Mason nodded. 'Yes, boss. Jan Ross confirmed he wore a full-face balaclava. As you know, we spoke to the others. Alice Cairns thinks he might have been wearing one.'

'And the knife's a constant in all three cases,' Lyall said. 'Jan Ross thinks it was a stiletto.'

'She saw it?' Knox asked.

'Only for a brief moment,' Mason said. 'She described it as thin – half the length of a bread knife.'

'And the attacker, her description tallies with the CCTV images from the bank at George IV Bridge?'

'Pretty much. Jan thinks he was behind her when she crossed the pedestrian lights from Middle Meadow Walk to the path at Fingal Place. Gave his height as five-seven or eight.'

'She wasn't aware of him before then?'

'No,' Lyall said. 'She glanced back as she crossed Argyle Place. When he saw her, he began speaking into a mobile phone. She assumed he was talking to someone.'

'Hmm,' Knox said. 'Safe to say it's the same man. We'll have confirmation when we get the DNA results.' He glanced back at the whiteboard and placed the tip of the marker at the second name. 'Alice Cairns. Anything new there?'

'Only that her stair door doesn't have a properly functioning key,' Mason said. 'As you know, she was attacked in the stairwell, which was unlit. A dud bulb.'

'Yvonne and I think he'd been watching her for a day or two,' Lyall said. 'Knew where she stayed and was waiting either in or near the block where she lives. Maybe even disabled the light.'

'So an element of planning went into it?' Knox said. 'Unlike Jan Ross, who appears to be random?'

'Just a hunch, boss,' Lyall said. 'But we think so.'

'Sometimes a hunch is all you need,' Knox said, indicating the third name. 'And Rachel Miller?'

'Similarity with Alice Cairns,' Mason said. 'She too had done some shopping on the way home. Her flat was in darkness when she arrived back and she was reaching for the hall switch when the attacker pounced.'

Lyall nodded in agreement. 'He slammed the door behind him, cutting out light from the stair. She can't be positive, but she doesn't think he was wearing a mask.'

'And she heard no one prior to that?'

'No,' Mason said. 'But she did pass a neighbour on her way home. A Mrs Cuthbert, who stays at the flat above. Kate and I thought it possible her attacker had loitered outside, waiting for one of the occupants to leave. Which was how he gained access.'

'You spoke to Mrs Cuthbert?'

'Yes. We respected Rachel's confidentiality, of course. Didn't mention the assault. We told her we were investigating break-ins in the area.'

'And did she see anyone?'

'No, nobody.'

'She was concerned about security, though,' Lyall said. 'Apparently she's only recently taken the flat on a six-month lease. She told us she was out during the day.'

'You reassured her?'

'Yes,' Mason said, grinning. 'Carried out a free security check. Her door was fitted with a mortise deadlock, double cylinder. We advised her she'd little to worry about.'

'Anything else?' Knox asked.

'Yes,' Lyall said. 'Rachel did mention one other thing, which may prove irrelevant.'

'What was that?' Knox asked.

'The man who attacked her wore a particularly pungent aftershave.'

Knox shook his head. 'Doesn't seem relevant at this point, Kate, but you never know–'

The detectives' attention was suddenly diverted to the door, which opened at that moment and DI Murray entered carrying a folder. 'Afternoon, all,' he said.

'Afternoon,' Knox said, pointing to the file. 'The DNA results?'

Murray nodded and took a print-out from the folder. 'Yes,' he confirmed. 'Both cases.'

Knox accepted the paper and studied it for several moments. 'An analysis of the brick found at the World's End Close murder scene. It says: "Blood, hair and skin found confirms the broken edge of the brick was used to inflict the injuries which proved fatal. Multiple examples of precedent touch-DNA found on other surfaces. The most recent contact, however, deposited a significant amount of acrylonitrile and butadiene residue."' Knox shook his head in bewilderment. 'Translate that into English for me, will you, Ed?'

Murray grinned. 'The material used in the manufacture of nitrile gloves, Jack,' he said. 'The killer wore them. Touch-DNA found on the brick was deposited previously, probably weeks earlier. Most likely from builders handling it before it was thrown into the skip.'

'So, he came prepared?'

'Looks that way.'

Knox glanced back at the paper, then turned to Lyall and Mason. 'The last paragraph is on Jan Ross. DNA from the semen sample proves it's the same rapist.'

Mason and Lyall exchanged glances, then Mason said, 'You were right, Kate.'

Knox waved the paper and addressed Murray. 'Thanks for getting the results back this afternoon, Ed. Bummer about the gloves, but much appreciated.'

Murray dipped his head in acknowledgement and headed for the door. 'We're still testing the clothes Tuffnell wore, Jack. Fair chance something'll turn up there.'

As Murray departed, Knox glanced at his watch. 'Okay, folks,' he said. 'It's nearly six. Guess that'll do it for the day. We can pick it up again in the morning.'

* * *

Knox had been back in his flat for only ten minutes when his mobile rang. He checked the screen, pressed *accept*, and said, 'Yvonne?'

'Indian or fish and chips?'

'You're buying?'

'No, you miserable old git, you are. You can reimburse me when I get there.'

'Hey. Not so much of the *old*.'

'Well, I'll still be in my forties when you retire,' Mason said teasingly.

'Nasty.'

A giggle, then, 'Sorry.'

'Bickering like an old married couple,' Knox replied. 'And we're still only engaged.'

'Doesn't bode well, does it?' A pause. 'You haven't answered my question.'

'What?'

'Indian or fish and chips?'

'Where are you?'

'Back in the car. I've been picking up my mail.'

'Warrender Park Terrace?'

'Uh-huh.'

'So you're nearer Kamal's than the chippie?'

'Uh-huh.'

'Then it's an Indian.'

'Okay. You can pour me an Absolut. See you in fifteen minutes.'

* * *

After they'd finished their tandoori chicken, Mason took the plates to the kitchen and re-joined Knox on the sofa. 'What kind of man do you think he is?' she said.

Knox took a sip of Glenmorangie and returned his glass to the coffee table. 'The rapist?'

'Yes.'

'You mean psychologically?'

'Mm-hmm,' Mason said. 'I'm trying to get a picture. Whether he finds it difficult to have a normal relationship with a woman, for example. Perhaps he can't find intimacy that way, because he has a hang-up about his appearance or has limited social skills. Or maybe it's just a power thing?'

Knox shook his head. 'Some of those factors, I guess, or a combination of all of them. I'm no expert, but I've read reports which suggest it can be hard to pinpoint. He could be a guy who seems perfectly normal. Or, conversely, an introverted loner. Others can be aroused only by subjugating their victim. Many of those cases – particularly where a weapon is involved – end up with an act of violence.'

'Our guy has a knife. You think he might use it?'

'He has a rudimentary knowledge of anatomy, knows where the carotid artery is. So far his victims have complied with his demands.' Knox paused. 'What if the next one doesn't?'

'Jeez.'

Knox put a reassuring arm around her shoulder. 'Don't worry, Yvonne. It's likely he'll trip himself up before it gets that far.'

Mason pursed her lips. 'I wish I could be sure.'

Knox rose and went to the drinks cabinet and poured a generous measure of Absolut. He brought it back to the table and said, 'I meant to tell you. Jamie phoned on Saturday. Confirmed our booking at the South View Hotel in Brisbane, December 27.'

Mason brightened. 'Hard to believe we'll be Mr and Mrs Knox by then.'

Knox sat down again, kissed her, and smiled. 'Better get used to it, Yvonne.'

Mason took a swallow of Absolut and began to reminisce. They'd been engaged for the better part of six months and were arranged to be married in Peebles on Christmas Eve.

Peebles, she reflected, Knox's home town. Where he'd started his career before transferring to St Leonards in 2002. He'd been married to his first wife then. He and Susan divorced in 2006, when she moved to Moreton Bay near Brisbane, where her sister lived.

Jamie, Knox's son, hadn't long gained his dentistry degree and he, together with wife Anne and daughter Lily, had gone to Australia to join Susan in 2014.

Knox and his ex remained on good terms. Mason had met her a couple of months earlier, when she returned to Scotland for her father's funeral, and they'd become friends. Susan knew Knox doted on Lily, and it was she who suggested they honeymoon in Brisbane.

Mason shucked off her shoes, drew her feet onto the sofa, and caressed his cheek. 'I'm almost used to it now, Jack,' she said. 'I spend almost as much time here as I do in Marchmont.'

'We agreed you'll move in permanently soon. You told me at the weekend you'd decide about your flat?'

'Whether to sell it or let, you mean?'

'Yes.'

Mason took a sip of vodka and replaced her glass on the table. 'I've made up my mind – I'll sell. After we're married, though; early next year, probably. No guarantee I'd get a buyer right away, anyway, so in the meantime I'm thinking of letting it.'

Knox nodded. 'Good idea. From what I hear there's fair demand for rental property. You'll have no bother finding a tenant. You've contacted a letting agency?'

'Not yet. But there's one at Bruntsfield which was recommended by neighbours. I'll give them a ring in the morning. Get something sorted.'

Chapter Ten

The tidy-looking blonde and her mousey-looking pal were talking to Myra the receptionist when he arrived. The girl looked as good as he remembered from yesterday: high cheekbones and pale-blue eyes; a pretty, dimpled chin, and a ready smile revealing perfect teeth.

The receptionist glanced up as he entered and nodded to a door at the rear of the office. 'You're late,' she said with a hint of admonishment. 'I think Mr Turnbull wants you to take these ladies to a property at Viewforth Square.'

'I know, Myra,' he replied. 'I checked it over yesterday. Made sure it was ready for occupancy.'

The door behind her opened at that moment and a tall, middle-aged man exited. 'Ah, there you are, Derek,' he said.

'Sorry, Mr Turnbull,' he said. 'Got caught in traffic at Tollcross. A double-decker bus broke down outside the King's Theatre and reduced Leven Street to a single lane.'

'Not to worry, you're here now, that's the main thing.' Turnbull motioned to the women. 'This is Ms Ania Joscowski and her friend, Ms Lidka Nowak. They've taken a six-month lease on the flat at Viewforth Square. They'd like to move in today.'

Tate saw the old creep give Ania on oily grin as he added, 'Subject to their approval, of course.' His boss cleared his throat and continued, 'You checked it out yesterday. All was fine?'

'Yes. Both electricity and gas were switched back on while I was there. Everything looks okay.'

'Good,' Turnbull said, and handed him the keys. 'Would you take the ladies up and settle them in?'

Derek Tate accepted the keys and smiled at the women, his eyes lingering on Ania. 'Of course, Mr Turnbull,' he said, then waved towards the door. 'Ladies?'

* * *

Knox's call to Frances Mainwaring had been answered by her son, Richard, who informed the detective that his mother had suffered a recent stroke.

Knox told him about Tuffnell, and asked if she was well enough to be interviewed.

'The left side of her face has been affected, but she can speak a little. You may not understand what she's saying, though.'

'I see, sir,' Knox replied. 'It's procedure, though, and necessary. Is it possible that you or someone else might be at home with her?'

'When would you be calling?'

'This morning, if it's convenient,' Knox said.

'Well, I'll be here for the remainder of the week, as it happens. Sometime before lunch?'

'That's fine, thanks. We're leaving Edinburgh now. Say eleven o'clock?'

'Very well. I'll let her know. We'll expect you then.'

The drive had taken just over an hour. Knox took the M9 exit just north of Stirling and glanced at the sat nav. 'We're almost there,' he said. 'Another six miles.'

Fulton looked over at the device. 'Abercorn Lodge,' he said. 'Sounds imposing.'

Knox approached a T-junction and indicated left. 'I suppose if you've a few hundred thou lying about and are able to take a punt on the stock market, you'd live in a nice manor, too.'

Fulton gave a reflective nod. 'Aye, boss, I suppose I would.'

They continued a few miles further, then Knox spotted a large sandstone villa set back off the road. It was approached by a long tarmacked driveway, its entrance flanked by a pair of stone pillars, the left one of which bore the name, "Abercorn Lodge".

Knox turned into the drive and continued to a portico with oak-timbered doors. After they exited and Knox keyed the car's remote locking, one of the doors opened and a sandy-haired man in his mid-forties came out and extended his hand. 'Richard Mainwaring,' he said.

'Our surname's often mispronounced,' he explained, 'but it's the same as the Arthur Lowe character in *Dad's Army*. You'll be Detective Inspector Knox?'

'Yes,' Knox replied. 'And this is Detective Sergeant Fulton.'

They shook hands, then Mainwaring waved to the door. 'Mother's in the drawing room. Will you come this way?'

They followed him through a wide reception hall and along a hallway into a front-facing room where a bay window overlooked the lawn. An elderly woman was sitting in a winged leather armchair in front of an ornate fireplace with a wood-burning stove.

She looked up as the detectives entered, and Knox became aware of her pale-green eyes giving them a searching appraisal.

'Mother,' Mainwaring said. 'This is–'

'You already told me who they were,' she replied. The left side of her face sagged a little, but her speech was only slightly slurred. 'I suffered a stroke, Richard,' she went on, 'I haven't gone senile.'

Her son gave her a chastened look. 'Sorry, Mother.'

Mrs Mainwaring straightened in her armchair and studied Knox for a moment. 'My son tells me Tuffnell was found dead?'

'Yes, ma'am.'

'Where, if you don't mind my asking?'

'Edinburgh's High Street. World's End Close at the Netherbow to be exact.'

Mrs Mainwaring raised her eyebrows. 'World's End Close?'

'Yes, ma'am. Near the foot of the High Street.'

The woman took a pink patterned handkerchief from her lap and dabbed the corner of her mouth. 'Yes,' she said. 'Yes, I know where it is. You're sure he was murdered?'

'Yes, ma'am. We've good reason to believe so.'

Mrs Mainwaring gave a barely discernible shake of the head, then waved to some chairs positioned near the window. 'Richard, please, fetch the gentlemen a seat.'

Her son took three chairs, arranged them near his mother's armchair, then gestured for the detectives to sit down. As Knox and Fulton did so, he said, 'Would you like a coffee? Inspector Knox, Sergeant Fulton?'

Knox glanced at Fulton, who dipped his head in agreement. 'If you don't mind, sir, yes, that would be very much appreciated.'

Mainwaring went to the hallway and called out, 'Mary!'

A moment later a plump woman wearing a white pinafore appeared at the door. 'Yes, sir?' she said.

'Could you bring us a large pot of coffee and a plate of biscuits, please. Four cups.'

'Not for me, Richard,' Mrs Mainwaring said, then turned to Knox. 'My medication,' she explained. 'Coffee and pills appear to stimulate my bladder.'

Her son cleared his throat and gestured towards the door. 'Mary shouldn't be long.'

Mrs Mainwaring ignored her son's embarrassment. 'I suppose we should get to the point of your visit,' she said. 'My association with Tuffnell. You know about the other investors – Mr Denison and Mr Coutts? That we took him to court and lost our case?'

'Yes, ma'am,' Knox replied. 'We talked to Christine Dalrymple and Brigadier Coutts.'

Mrs Mainwaring shook her head. 'I told the Denisons it was pointless. My late husband was a barrister and I've a little knowledge of the law. The case rested on a telephone conversation in which Tuffnell vouchsafed the game to be the Wylies' own invention. A statement he knew was false and later denied having made.' She gave a deep sigh and continued, 'But then I never trusted Tuffnell.'

There was a knock at the door and the plump woman entered carrying a tray, which she placed on a nearby coffee table.

Richard Mainwaring turned to the detectives. 'You both take milk and sugar?'

Knox replied for himself and Fulton, 'Please, two spoons.'

'The same for me, Mary, please,' Mainwaring said.

The woman spooned sugar and added milk, then gave the three men their coffee and left. Mainwaring cradled his cup and saucer in his lap and nodded to the table. 'Just help yourselves to biscuits.'

Fulton gave an enthusiastic nod and reached over and took a couple. 'Thank you, sir,' he said. 'Don't mind if I do.'

Knox took a sip of the coffee. 'You were saying, ma'am, that you didn't trust Mr Tuffnell,' he said. 'Yet you invested in NewTech?'

'It was because of Fairborough,' Mrs Mainwaring replied. 'You see, my husband began investing in the firm because he knew Fraser Noble and trusted him. He'd handled our account over the years and had advised us well. My husband had passed away by the time of Mr

Noble's illness, however, and Fairborough was looking after our account. He introduced Tuffnell when he was brought in to take over Fraser's clients.'

She leaned forward and gave Knox an earnest look. 'Did you ever meet anyone, Inspector, whom you distrusted immediately?' Her mouth trembled suddenly and she gave a little laugh.

'Isn't that silly? As a detective of course you must have. You know what I mean, though?' She placed a hand on her midriff. 'You feel it in here – a complete lack of rapport. I told Fairborough to close my account.'

The slackness on the left side of Mrs Mainwaring's face was more noticeable and her speech had become less coherent. She waved towards her son. 'Explain, Richard, please,' she said.

'What my mother's saying is that we gave notice we were pulling our account when Tuffnell came on board,' he said. 'Sir Michael apologised, and promised he would personally continue to oversee our investments if we'd reconsider.'

'Your mother did?'

'Yes, she agreed, and a month later he came to us with the NewTech deal, which he recommended. It seemed particularly promising, so we went ahead.'

'You knew about the other investors?' Knox asked.

'Mr Denison and Brigadier Coutts? Yes.'

'Did Sir Michael Fairborough explain that Mr Tuffnell was involved?'

'Yes, but he said Tuffnell would only represent the two other clients. He told my mother he would oversee our investment himself.'

'Did he say anything when Edward Denison discovered NewTech's breach of copyright?'

'No. It was Edward Denison who contacted me directly. I believe he also spoke to Brigadier Coutts.'

Mrs Mainwaring's hands became animated, and she said something Knox didn't understand.

'Mother says she spoke to Fairborough immediately after Edward told us,' her son said. 'But he gave every assurance there was no infringement of copyright.'

The detectives exchanged glances. 'So he backed up the claim Tuffnell made to Edward Denison?' Knox said.

'Yes.'

'Didn't you call Sir Michael to testify in the case against Mr Tuffnell?'

'We approached him before we went to court. But by then he insisted he'd also been duped into believing Tuffnell had seen the games.'

Again Mrs Mainwaring spoke for several moments, after which her son nodded in understanding.

'Mother confirms there was little point calling him to court as there was nothing in writing. However, she believes Fairborough to be every bit as much a charlatan as Tuffnell. She also said to let you know we've transferred all of our investments to another firm.'

Knox dipped his head in acknowledgement and turned to Mrs Mainwaring. 'Thank you very much, ma'am,' he said. 'You've been very helpful.'

She gave a feeble smile and replied a little more lucidly. 'You're welcome, Inspector.'

The detectives rose and said goodbye, and her son escorted them to the car. 'My mother has been very stoical about her illness,' he said. 'But I believe the stress caused by Tuffnell's duplicity was a major factor in her stroke.'

'When did it happen, sir?' Knox asked.

'July,' Mainwaring said. 'A month after Mr Denison took his life. Two events; one contributory factor.' He shook his head. 'You know, Inspector, we investors lost a fortune, but not Tuffnell or Fairborough. On the contrary, they took almost two hundred grand in commission before NewTech received its first penny.'

'And Mr Tuffnell,' Knox said. 'You saw him after the court case?'

Mainwaring gave a little smile. 'Have I an alibi for the time he was murdered, you mean?'

'If you're able to tell us that, sir, it would be helpful.'

'I'm in the travel business, Inspector. Arranging accommodation for foreign tour groups visiting Edinburgh. The high end of the market – four and five star hotels. I was at a meeting with hoteliers at the Balmoral Hotel in Princes Street, where I stayed until yesterday morning. After dinner, a half dozen of us had a drink in the bar. I retired shortly before midnight, as their night receptionist will verify. She handed me my room key.'

Chapter Eleven

'What do you think, boss?' Fulton was saying. 'Richard Mainwaring's story sounds plausible?' He and Knox had re-joined the M9, and were on their way back to Edinburgh.

'We'll check it out, of course,' Knox said. 'His mother, though. I think we may have received a clue that she knows something she's not telling.'

'Really?' Fulton said. 'I missed that.'

'At the start of the interview, when I told her where Tuffnell's body was found. She gave a slight shake of her head. As if she found it hard to believe.' He shrugged. 'Maybe she was annoyed I'd assumed she didn't know where it was.'

'I also thought it a coincidence,' Fulton said, 'that Mrs Mainwaring and Christine Dalrymple both took an instant dislike to Tuffnell the first time they met him.'

'Uh-huh, that thought struck me, too. And their instincts proved right.'

'Aye,' Fulton mused. 'Female intuition.'

'The other thing was that Fairborough lied. He claimed the NewTech investors were all Tuffnell's clients. Failed to mention he'd handled the Mainwaring account himself.'

'Or that he knew there was a question over copyright.'

'Yeah,' Knox said. 'Curious.'

'We'll be having another word?'

'Definitely.'

Knox keyed in a number on his phone on the dashboard. 'Meantime I'll give Edward Denison a bell. See if we can set up an interview.'

The ring tone sounded over the speakers, and moments later a woman's voice answered, 'Hello?'

Knox glanced at his watch and saw it was three minutes to twelve. 'Good morning,' he said. 'Would it be possible to speak to Mr Edward Denison, please?'

'I'm sorry,' the woman replied. 'My husband's at his office. Who's calling?'

'Detective Inspector Knox, Gayfield Square Police Station. I take it that's Mrs Denison?'

'Yes, Jennifer Denison. Why do you want to speak to him?'

'It's in connection with the death of a Mr Adrian Tuffnell. I believe your husband had dealings with him?'

'Yes, he sold my father-in-law shares in a company called NewTech.'

'You mentioned he was at the office, Mrs Denison. Would that be in Edinburgh?'

'Yes. My husband's an account director with Galton and Smeaton Advertising, 31 Melville Square.' A pause, then, 'He'll be breaking for lunch shortly. Would you like his direct number?'

'Please, if you wouldn't mind.'

After Mrs Denison read it to him, Knox thanked her and redialled, and a moment later a man's voice answered, 'Edward Denison?'

'Good afternoon, Mr Denison. My name is Detective Inspector Knox. We're investigating the death of a man we believe you had dealings with: Mr Adrian Tuffnell. I was wondering if it was possible to speak with you sometime this afternoon?'

'You called me at home? My wife let you have this number?'

'Yes, sir.'

'M-hmm,' Denison said. 'Okay. I'm having lunch with a client at twelve-thirty. I can see you at my office at 2pm. You know where it is?'

'Yes, sir. Mrs Denison gave us the address.'

'Fine. I'll tell the receptionist to expect you.'

Denison rang off and Fulton said, 'He didn't seem surprised to receive your call.'

'He didn't, did he?' Knox said. 'I wonder why.'

* * *

'It's very spacious,' Ania Joscowski was saying. He had driven with the girls the short distance to Viewforth Square and was showing them around the flat.

He nodded agreement and took them into the bathroom. 'Yes,' he said. 'Late Victorian. Built between the 1870s and 1900.' He pointed upwards and added, 'You can tell by the high ceilings. Quite common in buildings of the period.'

Ania's friend, Lidka, gazed at the carved cornices above the modern fitted shower. 'Yes,' she said. 'It gives a feeling of spaciousness.'

He studied the shorter of the two women for a moment. She wore a pair of tortoise shell glasses and looked quite studious. 'You speak English well,' he said. 'You've been in Scotland long?'

Ania gave a little laugh. 'Only two years,' she said. 'But we took English at Poznań University, the city where we come from.'

Her friend dipped her head in agreement. 'We came to Edinburgh to work with my brother Joseph, who runs a delicatessen in Morningside. He intends opening another shop in Leith, so we're learning the business. We hope to be able to manage it for him.'

They walked through to the kitchen as she spoke where the women appraised the fixtures. Ania pointed to the cooker. 'The oven, Mr…' She paused. 'Sorry, I forgot to ask you your name?'

'Derek,' he said. 'Derek Tate.'

Ania nodded. 'The oven, Mr Tate – is it electric, or gas?'

'Gas,' Tate replied. 'Everything else is electric, though. Including the central heating.'

They moved into the smaller of the two bedrooms, where Ania went to the window and gazed outside. 'Front-facing, Lidka,' she said.

Tate gave her a mystified look.

'My friend isn't a good sleeper,' she explained. 'The sound of traffic keeps her awake at night. The other bedroom, Mr Tate, it faces the rear?'

Christ, he thought, his plans were beginning to unravel. 'No – no, this is really not a noisy area. I'm sure it wouldn't disturb your friend. The other room faces the rear, it's true. But it looks on to a back court. Lots of folk cutting grass, kids playing and the like. I'm sure the front room would be better for your friend.'

Ania smiled. 'We're out most of the day, Mr Tate, so that wouldn't be a problem. It's night-time that concerns us. No, I think the back room would suit Lidka better.'

The girls entered the larger of the two bedrooms and went to the window, where Ania turned to her diminutive friend. 'Lidka,' she said, 'you prefer it?'

The smaller girl nodded, and gave Ania a beseeching look. 'You really don't mind?'

'Of course not, *drogi przyjacielu*,' she replied. 'I'm perfectly happy with the room at the front.'

The women smiled, then embraced each other and lapsed into a fit of giggles.

Meanwhile Tate fumed inwardly and considered the change of circumstances. *Okay*. He wouldn't let it make any difference. He'd still access the flat via the back bedroom window, and pray that Ania's mousy little pal did indeed sleep better in the absence of traffic.

* * *

Mason and Lyall were checking the rape case files when forensics officer DS Liz Beattie arrived with an update. 'Jan Ross's attacker,' she said. 'Your report mentioned that one of the victims thought he wore aftershave?'

'Yes,' Lyall confirmed. 'Rachel Miller.'

Beattie took a sheet of A4 paper from an envelope and laid it on Lyall's desk. 'We found a thread in the clump of bushes where Ms Ross was raped. We think it's from the balaclava her attacker wore. The lab subjected it to analysis and discovered it's a brand called Knight Errant.'

Lyall looked over the forensics report, which she handed to Mason. 'Obscure make,' she said. 'Never heard of it.'

Hathaway glanced up from his desk, where he was studying a transcript of Knox and Fulton's interview with Coutts. 'It's a supermarket brand, I think,' he said. 'I'm sure I've seen it in Lidl or Aldi, somewhere like that.'

'Something to keep on file, I guess,' Mason said. 'Might prove helpful in the long run.'

'DI Murray gave you the DNA results last night?' Beattie asked Lyall. 'Cairns, Miller and Ross; same rapist?'

Lyall nodded. 'Yes,' she said, nodding to her computer screen. 'Yvonne and I were just going over the victims' statements. Trying to finesse a profile on the guy.'

'Anything stand out?'

'Well, Jan Ross was the only one to get a half-decent look, but even so it was dark. Still, between what she saw and CCTV images from a bank in George IV Bridge, we know he's of average build, dark-haired and around five seven or eight.'

'Fairly well-spoken, too,' Mason said. 'Very likely middle-class.'

'Yeah,' Lyall agreed. 'He's intelligent. Knows where the main artery in the neck is located, and what it's called.'

'We're also guessing he lives in Edinburgh,' Mason said. 'Or at least works here. He drives, and has a car. Rachel Miller stays in Leith and Alice Cairns in Joppa. Fair distance between both assaults.'

'You think he's likely to strike again soon?' Beattie asked.

Lyall gestured to the desktop. 'Bit of a pattern developing,' she said. 'Alice Cairns was the first of the current wave – August 14. Rachel Miller a fortnight later, August 29, and Jan Ross on Monday.'

'You said *current* wave,' Beattie said. 'There've been other incidents?'

'Not where an actual rape took place, no,' Lyall said, tracing her finger down the computer screen. 'But three reports from women who were followed by a man fitting our guy's description have been logged in the last four months. One in Newhaven where the girl was positive she'd been shadowed all the way from North Junction Street – a distance of just under a mile. Her stalker disappeared when her mother drove by and picked her up.'

'And the coincidence there,' Mason said, 'is that, like Jan Ross, at one point when the girl glanced back, he began speaking into his phone.'

'That was in May,' Lyall said. 'A month before that, on April 18, a nineteen-year-old called Tania Stevens was returning to her home in Abbeyhill after a night out with friends. A man grabbed her from behind and attempted to pull her into a side street. The girl's screams caught the attention of a man walking his dog, who shouted out. Her attacker took to his heels and ran off.'

'The next incident was on the ninth of June,' Mason said. 'In central Edinburgh. A young American tourist reported a man who had followed her from the Lawnmarket. When she continued down the enclosed steps from Victoria Terrace to Victoria Street he stayed with her. There's a turn in the stairs halfway down – a blind spot. He made a grab for her there but she knocked away his arm and hurried down to the street, where she called for help. Two men leaving a restaurant ran back up the steps, but her attacker had disappeared.'

'So it could be a sequence of attacks,' Beattie said. 'April to September?'

'We think so,' Lyall said. 'Nothing in July but that's not surprising. There might have been attacks which have gone unrecorded.'

Mason dipped her head in agreement. 'It's a sad fact, but many women don't report rapes. Either because they're ashamed, or are afraid we won't take them seriously.'

'So, you are saying you think he'll strike again?' Beattie said.

Lyall nodded to the screen. 'If these stats are anything to go by, yes,' she said.

Beattie shrugged and headed towards the door. 'You never know, he just might slip up.'

'Which is what we're hoping for,' Lyall said and held up the report. 'Thanks for dropping this off, Liz.'

'You're welcome,' Beattie said. 'See you later.'

As Beattie departed and Lyall and Mason went back to their computers, Hathaway picked up his telephone and dialled a number.

Moments later a voice replied. 'Muirfield Golf Club, members' lounge, Andrew Cafferty speaking.'

'Good afternoon,' Hathaway replied. 'Detective Constable Hathaway, Gayfield Square Police Station, Edinburgh. I'm calling in connection with one of your regulars, Brigadier Reginald Coutts.'

'Yes, sir,' Cafferty replied. 'I know the gentleman.'

'Brigadier Coutts was interviewed by our officers yesterday, and has stated he was in your members' lounge from approximately 9pm until 11.30pm on Monday evening. I wondered if you were able to confirm?'

There was a short silence on the phone, then Cafferty said, 'I'm checking the staff rota book, sir. Trying to find out who's on late duty this week. Ah, here we are – Pete Loughborough attends the section where Brigadier Coutts normally sits.'

'Mr Loughborough's on duty?' Hathaway asked.

'Yes,' Cafferty said. 'He starts at twelve. It's almost quarter past now.'

'Could you ask him to verify he served Brigadier Coutts?'

'Of course, sir. Between nine and eleven-thirty, you say?'

'Yes.'

'Just a moment. I'll ring his extension.'

Hathaway waited half a minute, then Cafferty came back on the line. 'Yes, sir, Pete confirms Brigadier Coutts was at his usual table between those times on Sunday evening.'

'You've misunderstood me,' Hathaway said. 'I was asking about Monday evening. 9th September?'

'Oh, sorry. Hang on a moment.' Another short silence, then, 'No, sorry, sir. He tells me the Brigadier wasn't in at all on Monday evening.'

'He's sure?'

'Yes, sir,' Cafferty said. 'I told him it was a police inquiry. He's a hundred per cent certain. Brigadier Coutts wasn't registered to play a round on Monday evening. Pete tells me he assigned his usual table to a couple of American guests.'

Chapter Twelve

'My sister phoned me yesterday,' Edward Denison was saying. 'Told me you'd interviewed her at my father's house.'

Knox and Fulton sat facing him at the opposite side of a large oak desk in his office at Galton and Smeaton Advertising in Melville Square. Denison was tall and distinguished-looking, and had an authoritarian demeanour.

'We did, sir, yes,' Knox said.

'So you'll be in possession of the facts of our dealings with Tuffnell. His dishonesty? That we took him to court and lost our case?'

'Yes, sir. Your sister made us aware of that.'

'Then I don't know what more I can tell you.'

'You know Mr Tuffnell was found dead in a close off the High Street early yesterday morning?'

'Yes. I wasn't surprised when you phoned me. Christine advised you're treating it as murder?'

'We are, sir, yes.'

'And I suppose the fact that she and I are among a group of people with a particular grievance against Tuffnell, automatically makes us suspects?'

Knox gave the hint of a smile. 'We *are* obliged to eliminate you from our inquiries, sir.'

'Which no doubt brings us to your next question, where were we when Tuffnell met his end?'

'Yes.'

'Then I can speak for us both,' Denison said. 'My wife Jennifer and I were having dinner with Christine and her husband, Phillip Dalrymple. Phillip is head of marketing at Greystone Distillers in Leith. We were celebrating the renewal of his company's advertising with Galton and Smeaton.'

'Where was this, sir?' Knox asked.

'The Forth Cutter Restaurant at the Shore in Leith.'

'And you were there all evening?'

'Yes,' Denison said. 'Greystone's chauffeur drove us home around 11.30pm. My sister and I live in Colinton, not far from one another. The driver must have dropped us off around midnight.'

'I see,' Knox said. 'Finally, sir, I'd like to ask about Mr Lawson, the gentleman who told you that the Wylies' game might be a rip-off.'

'Arthur Lawson. He and I were at George Heriot's together.'

'Mr Lawson has an interest in a company called TayImage?'

'Yes, they market a series of sports-orientated games.'

'I believe it was Mr Lawson who told you about NewTech's earlier breach of copyright – the Wylies copied a game from a firm called ADL studios?'

'Yes. One of the directors knew their father. The case was settled out of court.'

'You say Mr Lawson has an interest in TayImage. Are you aware if he has any involvement with ADL?'

Denison shrugged. 'From what I understand, the games industry is a fairly incestuous business. He may have. Why do you ask?'

Knox ignored the question. 'What was the game NewTech plagiarised, do you know?'

'I do, as a matter of fact,' Denison replied. '*Hired Guns*, an action game about a group of mercenaries in the tropics. One of their best sellers.'

Knox gave a nod of acknowledgement. 'And Mr Lawson. He's based in Dundee?'

Denison reached into his pocket, retrieved an address book, and leafed through the pages. 'No, he's here in Edinburgh. Runs a company called DD Enterprises. Would you like his details?'

'Yes, sir, if you wouldn't mind. It might prove helpful.'

* * *

The Polish girls signed the lease, and he handed over the keys and left them to it.

He mulled it over as he returned to his car. Things hadn't turned out as he'd planned, but after giving it some thought, his new scenario might prove as good as any.

He'd wait until the wee hours – 3am or thereabouts, when he was sure he could access the flat without rousing Ania's mate. The bedroom doors might be closed, but it was unlikely they'd be locked, so he could easily flit from one bedroom to the other.

He'd already undertaken a recce of surrounding properties, and saw no obstacle to an intruder entering from the rear. A series of low walls separated the gardens, but they would be easily surmounted. After that it was just a matter of shinning up the fire escape, and hey presto…

Except he wouldn't be climbing any walls. He had a copy of the door keys, which he'd use to access the back court. He'd lock it from behind, and leave the property the same way. He reckoned his liaison would only take minutes, then, with Ania threatened into silence, he'd be out of the flat and away before the alarm was raised.

His mobile phone rang as he clicked his seat belt into place, and he glanced at the screen and answered, 'Mr Turnbull?'

'Everything okay, Derek?' his boss said. 'The Polish girls liked the flat? They completed the contract?'

'Aye, they liked it fine. It's signed and I've given them the keys.'

'Good work. I thought it would be just a formality.' A slight pause, then, 'Where are you now?'

'Still at Viewforth Square. Just got back to the car.'

'That's ideal.' He heard the rustle of paper and Turnbull continued, 'We've just received a query from a woman in Warrender Park Terrace. Intends putting her flat up for lease next month and wants us to handle it. She works, but says she'll be at the property this lunchtime: twelve-thirty till one-thirty. Will you go over and see her?'

Tate checked his watch: 12.25pm. Warrender Park Terrace was only a ten-minute drive away. 'Certainly, Mr Turnbull,' he said. 'I'll head over there now.'

'Excellent,' Turnbull said. 'Myra's texting you her name and address now. Oh, by the way, I've explained we'll need a copy of the keys if she decides to go ahead.'

Tate's phone pinged at that moment and he glanced at the text. 'Got it, Mr Turnbull.'

'Okay, Derek. I'll leave it with you.'

It took just under eight minutes for Tate to cover the three-quarters of a mile from Viewforth Square to Warrender Park Terrace. He checked his phone for the prospective client's name as he exited his car: Ms Yvonne Mason.

He mounted a short flight of stairs, studied the names next to the intercom, and thumbed the buzzer. Seconds later, a woman's voice answered, 'Hello?'

'Ms Mason?'

'Yes.'

'Derek Tate, ATN Property Management. You spoke earlier to Mr Turnbull, my boss?'

'Oh, yes,' Mason replied. 'Come on up.'

A buzzer sounded and Tate pushed the door and ascended the stairs to the third floor, where a young woman waited at the end of the landing. She looked a year or two older than he was; late twenties or early thirties. She had an attractive face, a trim figure, and collar-length auburn hair.

She smiled and waved him into the flat. 'Thanks for arriving so promptly. I was in the process of making coffee. Can I get you one?'

'I wouldn't mind, thanks,' Tate replied.

'You take sugar?'

'Two, please.'

He followed her along a short hallway into the living room, where she pointed to an armchair. 'Take a seat,' she said, then nodded towards the kitchen. 'It's freshly percolated. I'll only be a minute.'

He watched her exit, taking particular interest in her pert backside and shapely legs. A couple of minutes later she reappeared with two cups, set one on a table in front of him, then took a seat on a sofa opposite and held the other in her hand. 'I'd like to put it on the market at the end of the month. I currently live with my fiancé and I'm hardly ever here.'

'I understand,' Tate said, then opened a briefcase at his feet and extracted a notebook. 'Okay – I'd better make some notes,' he said. 'The property has two bedrooms?'

Mason dipped her head in confirmation. 'Two bedrooms, a kitchen and bathroom, three large cupboards.'

'Shower or bath?'

'Shower.'

Tate held up his iPhone. 'I'll take some photos of the rooms before I go,' he said. 'Gives prospective tenants an idea of what the property looks like. You don't mind?'

'No, not at all.'

'Good,' Tate replied, then returned the phone to his pocket and began writing in his notepad. 'And of course you're central, that's a plus. Lots of professional folk work in the centre of Edinburgh.' He took a long swallow of his coffee and went on, 'Now, rental. Naturally, we ask the lessee for six months in advance. You've an idea what you'd be asking for?'

Mason shrugged. 'Hadn't given it a great deal of thought, to be honest. What's the going rate?'

Tate looked up from his notebook. 'I think £1,200 per calendar month is fair. You'd be okay with that?'

'Sounds fine.'

'We'd need duplicate keys, too. Allows us to show the flat to prospective tenants.'

'No problem,' Mason said. 'I've a spare set. I'll let you have them before you go.'

Tate closed his notebook, put it back in his briefcase, and took out his mobile. 'Right,' he said. 'That just leaves the pictures.'

Mason nodded to his cup. 'You've finished your coffee?'

'Yes, thanks.'

'Okay,' Mason said, then placed her own cup on the table and stood up. 'I'll give you the guided tour.'

Tate followed her through each of the other rooms, taking pictures from different angles. When they'd finished, he said, 'Okay, the cupboards.'

Mason rolled her eyes. 'Mostly stuff I never got around to unpacking.'

'Don't worry,' he reassured her. 'It's only to give tenants an idea of storage space.'

Mason walked to the end of the hallway and opened the first of three cupboards, which was empty save for a dozen large cardboard boxes. Tate pressed the shutter button, and the flash activated and took the picture. He did the same at the adjoining cupboard, in which were an assortment of mops, pails, brushes and a cylinder vacuum cleaner.

Mason turned to the third cupboard. 'I use this as an overflow wardrobe,' she said. 'It's where I keep items of clothing I seldom use.'

She opened the door, and the first thing Tate saw was a uniform in a clear garment bag at the front of a rail. He glanced to the shelf above, and spotted the chequer-banded hat that went with it.

Mason reached over, took the uniform and hung it behind a coat further back, then took the hat off the shelf and stood back. 'I don't think we should include those in the picture,' she said. 'Might be a little off-putting.'

Tate stared at her for a long moment, then found his voice. 'You're a policewoman?'

'Detective Constable, CID,' Mason replied, and pointed to the rack. 'Dress uniform, all plain-clothes officers are required to have one. Like I said, seldom used.'

'Oh.'

'So,' Mason said, looking at him directly. 'This'll be your last one?'

'Huh?' Tate said, suddenly uneasy.

She gestured to the cupboard. 'The picture?'

'Oh… I see,' he replied, and raised his iPhone and framed the photo. 'Yes,' he added, clicking the shutter. 'This should be enough.'

Chapter Thirteen

'Getting to be a fair number of suspects,' Knox said as he steered his Passat into Queensferry Street.

'Arthur Lawson, boss,' Fulton said. 'I was wondering why you were interested.'

'Curiosity,' Knox replied. 'Had he an axe to grind?'

'You think NewTech's lifting of ADL's game affected him financially?'

Knox nodded. 'You heard Denison say the business was incestuous. So, aye, it's possible. He knew the Wylies were on thin ice with *Armageddon 2*. Which begs the question: how did the Yanks discover their game had been cloned?'

'Lawson blew the whistle?'

Knox shrugged but said nothing.

'The Wylies had a motive, too,' Fulton said. 'If they believed Tuffnell brought about their downfall.'

'Exactly. Like I said, quite a list.'

'The Denisons' alibi appears sound enough.'

'Only if they were where they claim to be.'

'You'll do a CCTV check?'

'Bound to be something covering the Forth Cutter Restaurant at the Shore.'

Knox placed his iPhone on the hands-free unit on the dash, keyed a number, and added, 'I'll ring Hathaway, get the ball rolling.'

Hathaway's voice came through the speakers when the call connected. 'Boss?'

'Mark,' Knox said. 'You checked on Coutts?'

'I did, boss,' Hathaway replied. 'He was telling porkies.'

'He wasn't in the Muirfield Club's bar on Monday night?'

'No. The last time they saw him was twenty-four hours earlier. Sunday 8th September.'

'Brass-necked bugger,' Knox said. 'Okay, I'll get in touch again, bring him in for interview. Meantime I've a wee list I'd like you to make a start on.'

'Boss?'

'Christine and Edward Denison. Supposed to have been with their respective spouses at the Forth Cutter Restaurant at the Shore on Monday night. See if you can chase up local CCTV. Apparently they were chauffeured home, arriving around midnight. You know what they look like?'

'Only Edward Denison. I found a picture after Googling his ad agency. Not sure about his sister.'

'Slim,' Knox said. 'Five-two or three; dark shoulder-length hair.'

'Right.'

'And, Mark?'

'Uh-huh?'

'Check with reception at the Balmoral Hotel. See if they had a Mr Richard Mainwaring registered on Monday. If so, find out if staff can confirm he took his room key and retired at eleven-thirty. The time's important.'

'Boss.'

'One more thing. I'm also interested in Jason and Ross Wylie, bosses of NewTech, now bankrupt. See if you can locate their current whereabouts.'

'Righto, boss.'

Knox pulled into the kerb as Hathaway rang off, took out his notebook and checked it, and dialled another number. Several moments later a man answered, 'Yes?'

'Brigadier Coutts?' Knox asked.

'No, this is Andrew Turner, his manservant. The brigadier isn't here at the moment. May I ask who's calling?'

'Detective Inspector Knox.' A pause, then, 'Can you tell me where he is?'

'Yes,' Turner replied. '*En route* to Edinburgh. He departed half an hour ago.'

'Has he a mobile?' Knox asked.

'He does, yes. Hold on a moment and I'll get it for you.'

Half a minute later Turner passed on the number and Knox thanked him and redialled. A few moments passed, and the detectives heard the raspy timbre of Coutts' voice. 'Who's calling?' he said.

'Detective Inspector Knox, Brigadier Coutts. I phoned you at home. Mr Turner was kind enough to let me have your mobile number.'

Coutts harrumphed, then said, 'You're the policeman I spoke to yesterday? About Tuffnell?'

'Yes.'

'Then why are you calling me today?' he said indignantly. 'I told you all I know.'

'Bit of a discrepancy, sir.'

'Discrepancy?'

'Yes. You told us you were in the bar at Muirfield Golf Club of Monday evening. We checked, and you weren't.'

'Sorry. Got the dates mixed up. I was there on Sunday evening.'

'Brigadier Coutts,' Knox said. 'You do realise this is a murder inquiry. That giving false information is a serious offence?'

'*Misleading* information, officer. Like I say, I made a mistake.'

'Where are you now, sir?'

'Sorry, I don't understand.'

'Mr Turner told us you were driving to Edinburgh. Where exactly are you at this moment?'

A short silence, then, 'Milton Road. I'm on my way to my club in Abercromby Place.'

'That isn't too far from Gayfield Square Police Station,' Knox said. 'I wonder if you'd mind coming in to see us first?'

Another short silence. 'You're asking me, or telling me?'

'It's a request, sir. See if we can iron out the discrepancy in your statement.'

The sound of Coutts clearing his throat reverberated through the speakers. 'Very well. I'll be there in ten minutes.'

* * *

'I didn't deliberately attempt to mislead,' Coutts was saying. Fifteen minutes had passed and he was seated at a table in Interview Room 2 at Gayfield Square, and Knox and Fulton were sitting opposite. 'But I had my, ahem, reasons.'

'And what were they, sir?' Knox asked.

Coutts studied Knox for a long moment. 'I'm sixty-two years old, Detective. Lost my wife two years ago. Pancreatic cancer. After her death I decided I wouldn't get married again. I didn't want a life tied to some woman who lived for cooking, knitting, gardening or any other domestic activity.

'My wife Barbara was like that, and to be honest, although I loved her dearly, it was never me. I like the outdoors; hiking and camping, fishing and grouse-shooting.

'The problem with a man pursuing those activities and, to be realistic, getting on a bit, is that you seldom have the opportunity to bed a woman. I didn't want to marry again, but I'm still sexually active. So, what do you do?

'My solution is to pay. I see a woman every other week and spend the night with her. Monday evening until Tuesday morning.'

'In Edinburgh?' Knox said.

Coutts took a small square of paper from his pocket, unfolded it, and spread it out on the table. 'I've written down her name, address and contact details. I rang her before I came here. I mentioned Tuffnell's death, and asked if she would vouch my whereabouts. She assured me she would.'

Knox glanced at the paper, on which a local address was written. 'New Town Health Centre?' he said.

Coutts delved into the breast pocket of his jacket and removed a print-out receipt, which he handed over. 'Many of her clients are married,' he said. 'And, believe it or not, she takes credit cards. The name disguises the nature of the business, in case wives find a receipt or scrutinise a credit card statement. You can see the amount paid, together with time and date.'

Knox took both pieces of paper and held them up. 'You understand we'll have to verify this?'

'Of course,' Coutts said.

Knox inclined his head towards the door. 'Okay, sir, you can go on to your club. Thank you for your cooperation.'

* * *

'The head concierge at the Balmoral is going to get back to us,' Hathaway was saying. 'The night receptionist doesn't come on duty until 10pm. I said I'd give him a ring again in the morning.'

The DC, together with Knox, Fulton, Mason and Lyall, were back in the office discussing the day's events.

'Okay,' Knox said. 'Any luck with CCTV?'

Hathaway swung the monitor to face Knox, and clicked on an icon. 'Yes,' he said. 'There's an engineering works immediately opposite the restaurant, which, by the way, is an old ship permanently moored at the dockside. The firm copied a section of their recording from 11pm to 12pm and e-mailed it to me.'

A window on the screen opened, giving a wide-angle view of a section of cobbled street, and the promenade deck of a ship moored at the edge of the dock beyond.

The vessel was accessed via a broad gangway, over which a blue awning bore the legend, *Forth Cutter Restaurant,* and was bedecked with a ribbon of multi-coloured lights fringing the gangway and upper section of the ship's superstructure.

Hathaway scrolled through the tape, which showed customers exiting every few minutes. When a counter at the top-right of the window read 11.41pm, he paused the recording.

'There,' he said, pointing to the screen. 'Two couples leaving. Isn't that them?'

'Could be,' Knox said. 'Restart the tape, Mark.'

Hathaway did so and Knox saw four people cross to the shore. Christine Dalrymple and her husband, a stocky, balding man, were first to step off the gangplank, followed by Edward Denison and his wife, a buxom blonde wearing an off-the-shoulder dress.

They stopped at the front of the awning, and a moment later an S-class Mercedes came into view. A uniformed chauffeur exited, opened the off-side passenger door, and the couples got inside.

'The security people at the engineering firm switched to a second camera at this point,' Hathaway said, indicating the screen.

The viewpoint changed, the camera now giving a view to the south. The Mercedes drove off and continued through a set of traffic lights, remaining on the road running parallel with the Water of Leith.

'He's keeping to The Shore,' Fulton said. 'Towards Henderson Street and Bonnington Road. Right direction if he's headed to Colinton.'

Knox glanced at the counter at top right-hand corner of the video, which now read 11.49pm. He dipped his head in acknowledgement. 'Appears what Denison told us was true. He and his sister were nowhere near the High Street at midnight on Monday.'

He shrugged and addressed Hathaway, 'Thanks, Mark.' A pause, then, 'Any joy with the Wylies?'

'Yes, boss. I checked the bankruptcy file for NewTech and found the company was registered at 85 Craigfield Road, Dundee, which turns out to be their parents' place. I rang and their mother told me the brothers emigrated to Canada at the end of May, a month after the court case. They're staying with an uncle in Halifax, working with a software development company in an area called Burnside. I asked the RCMP to verify residential status, and received a quick reply. Both Jason and Ross have been domiciled in Nova Scotia since the thirty-first of May.'

Chapter Fourteen

Tate parked his car in St Peter's Place and checked his watch: 2.38am. It was just a short walk to Viewforth Square and the only folk he encountered was a young couple who crossed his path at the traffic lights at Gilmore Place. They appeared to be drunk and were heading in the direction of Tollcross.

The man said something and the girl laughed out loud, then her boyfriend joined in and they continued on their way.

Arriving at Viewforth Square minutes later, he approached the stair entrance and took out a set of keys. He glanced around, then, satisfied he wasn't being watched, let himself in and moved silently towards the well of the stair.

Tate unlocked the rear door and entered the back court, relocked it at the other side, and edged towards the fire escape. He paused for a moment, looking up to make sure no lights were visible at the second floor. Satisfied there weren't, he mounted the final section of the fire escape and began climbing the steps.

Within moments he arrived at the platform outside Nowak's window, where he paused. The curtains hadn't been drawn, and there was just enough light to enable him to make out her slight figure beneath the duvet.

He watched for any movement to indicate she might still be awake, but saw none, save for the slight rise and fall of the coverlet caused by her breathing.

Tate reached into his jacket and put on his balaclava mask, then took out his penknife, unfolded the blade, and ran his fingers along the outside of the window sash. Locating the gap between inner and outer frame, he inserted the blade and slid it along until it connected with metal. He worked the blade gradually until the catch swung open.

He refolded the blade, replaced the penknife in his pocket, and gripped the lower edge of the sash with the tips of his fingers and began to lift. He was relieved to find it moved freely and noiselessly. A slight breeze fluttered the curtain as he sat on the sill. He swung his legs over the threshold, felt his feet connect with the floor, and slipped inside.

He lowered the window and stood at the curtains until his eyes adjusted to the darkness. He could see Nowak's sleeping form much clearer now, and the steady rhythm of her breathing assured him she was sleeping soundly. He looked beyond the bed to the door and gave a sigh of relief. It was slightly ajar, and not having to open the handle was one less thing to worry about.

Tate moved towards the door, and was almost level with the bed when he placed his foot on a loose floorboard, which emitted a loud *creak*. Nowak stirred, mumbling something in Polish. Tate froze and cursed under his breath. Why the hell hadn't he made sure of the flooring the first time he checked the flat!

Nowak shuffled under the duvet for a moment, then gave a loud snore and her breathing settled into a rhythm. Tate kept going and, after what seemed an eternity, arrived at the door. He gave the handle a light tug, edged through the gap, and crossed to the other side of the hallway.

As he approached Ania's room he saw that her door, too, was open. Tate remained still for several seconds, listening for signs she mightn't be asleep, but heard nothing. He pushed gently on the door, then glanced inside.

Ania lay with her head facing the window opposite. The curtains were drawn, the only light from the LED of an alarm clock on the bedside table.

He advanced to the bed, reached into his pocket and took out a stiletto, and clicked the blade into place. In one quick movement, he pulled back the duvet and thrust the knife at the girl's throat.

'Don't move or say anything,' he commanded. 'I'll slit your throat if you do – understand?'

Now fully awake, Ania was aware of the intentions of the masked man attempting to manoeuvre his way on top of her. Seconds before he was able to carry this out, she took swift and decisive action.

Deflecting Tate's knife with a swing of her left hand, she delivered a blow to his neck with the right. He recoiled instantly and collapsed to the floor, losing grasp of the stiletto.

Ania rose and ran to the door. 'Lidka!' she shouted. 'Help! Someone's trying to rape me.'

The blow caused Tate to experience a momentary blackout. He regained consciousness hearing Ania's shout, and realised she'd run into the other bedroom. A moment later he heard Nowak's door slam and a key turn in the lock.

He stood up, pain lancing through his neck. Christ, he thought, that bitch inflicted some damage. Her hand felt like the edge of a fucking plank. He picked up the knife and staggered into the hallway, aware of a rising commotion. The women were jabbering loudly in Polish, and at one point he heard the word 'police'. They were bound to have a mobile in there, and it wouldn't be long until they dialled 999.

His original plan had been thwarted now. He had to leave by the front door, and quickly. Lurching along the hallway he tried to open it, but found the mortise's deadbolt had been secured.

Where the hell were the keys?

For a moment he wondered if they were in Ania's bedroom, then remembered when he'd shown the women around the flat he'd left them on a ledge near the door.

Tate fumbled about in semi-darkness for a few seconds, and finally located them.

He unlocked the door, fled down the stairs, and exited the block. He pulled off his balaclava and forced himself not to run. The streets remained quiet, however, and he arrived at his car without incident.

'What a disaster,' he muttered as he settled into the driving seat. 'What a bloody disaster.'

* * *

Sergeant Beth Lindsay met Lyall and Mason at the entrance to the stair at Viewforth Square shortly after nine. 'The call came in at 3.10am this morning,' she explained. 'Two officers from Torphichen Police station attended.'

'The girl confirmed he attempted to rape her?' Lyall asked.

'Yes,' Lindsay replied.

'And he had a knife?' Mason said.

'Yes, thin-bladed. I checked your report on the HOLMES 2 database. Your rapist carries a stiletto?'

Lyall nodded. 'Yes.'

'Fits with the girl's description,' Lindsay said.

'She managed to fight him off?' Mason asked.

'Clobbered him, apparently,' Lindsay said. 'Her name's Ania Joscowski, Polish, aged 23. In her native city of Poznań, she got a black belt in karate. She ran to her friend's bedroom afterwards, where they locked themselves in and dialled the nines. Her name is Lidka Nowak, aged 24.'

'No trace of Ania's attacker?'

Lindsay shook her head. 'He managed to find the key to the front door, which was locked. Let himself out and fled from the stair. Our lads arrived here at 3.19am. Two extra patrols were summoned and did a complete search of the area. No joy, I'm afraid.'

'Any idea how he accessed the property?' Lyall asked.

'Via Lidka's bedroom,' Lindsay said. 'Faces the back court. A fire escape is located near the window, where the attacker effected entry. We think he came in via Gilmore Place and scaled a couple of walls. After he'd climbed the fire escape, there's an old-style lock on the window which secures the inner and outer frame. We took a quick look and think he inserted a knife into the sash and prised open the catch. We didn't disturb anything, naturally.'

Mason dipped her head in acknowledgment. 'Yes, we received a message before we left the office. Forensics officer DS Liz Beattie will attend this morning and check for DNA and fingerprints.'

Lindsay thumbed over her shoulder. 'I can leave you to it, then?'

'The girls, they're up there now?' Lyall asked.

'Uh-huh,' Lindsay said. 'Second floor. I told them to expect you.'

Lyall acknowledged Lindsay with a nod and she and Mason went inside. A few moments later they had ascended the stairs and arrived at the flat, where Mason's press on the bell was answered by Nowak. She glanced at the detectives' warrant cards and said, 'You're the people the uniformed policewoman told me about?'

'Sexual Offences Liaison, yes,' Lyall replied. 'I'm DS Lyall and my colleague is DC Mason. You're Ania?'

Nowak opened the door and waved them inside. 'No, her friend, Lidka. Ania is in the living room.'

The detectives followed Nowak along the hall and into the living room, where Joscowski was sitting on a sofa. Mason could see the strain of her ordeal etched into her face. The detectives introduced themselves, then Mason said, 'How are you feeling, Ania?'

'Tired,' Joscowski said, then motioned to her friend. 'Neither of us slept very well.'

'I understand,' Lyall said. 'And I know you've spoken to other officers, but do you mind if we go over it again? I promise we won't keep you long. Is that okay?'

'Yes,' Joscowski replied.

Lyall turned to Nowak. 'Lidka?'

'Yes, it's okay.'

Lyall took out her notebook. 'Could I begin by asking you both when you were first aware of the intruder?'

Nowak studied Lyall for a long moment. 'You mean did I hear him before Ania called out to me?'

'Yes.'

Nowak shook her head. 'I'm normally quite a light sleeper,' she said. 'But I heard nothing until Ania shouted.'

Lyall nodded. 'Sergeant Lindsay told you we think the intruder came in through your bedroom window? He ascended the fire escape and manipulated the window lock?'

'She did. But I don't think I heard anything. Unless…'

'Yes?'

'I was in the middle of a dream. When I was a child back in Poznań I had a soft toy called *Piski* – the word means to squeak, which was a noise he made when you squeezed him. In my dream, I heard *Piski* again. One of your policemen discovered a loose floorboard in my bedroom this morning. It makes the same kind of noise. It may have been that I had heard.'

'You didn't know about the floorboard?'

'No, we're renting the flat. We only moved in yesterday.'

'I see,' Lyall said, then turned to her friend. 'Ania, you told Sergeant Lindsay you awoke to find the intruder at your bed?'

'No,' Joscowski replied. 'Not *at* the bed. On top of it.' She made a face and continued, 'He had thrown back the duvet and pulled down the bedsheet when I realised what was happening. I saw the knife then, inches from my neck. He threatened to cut my throat if I didn't do as he asked. I was half scared, half angry. I reacted.'

'You managed to deflect the knife and land a blow to his neck,' Mason said. 'What happened then?'

'He fell to the floor and dropped the knife, I think,' Joscowski said. 'I got out of bed and shouted for Lidka. She took me into her bedroom and locked the door behind me.'

'And the intruder, you heard him after that?'

'Yes,' Nowak said. 'He sounded–' She paused and turned to Joscowski. '*Osłabiony*?'

'Weakened.'

'Yes, weakened. He stumbled about for a minute.'

'He was looking for the keys,' Joscowski said. 'The door to the flat was locked and the hall was in darkness. I don't think he knew where the light switch was, and he struggled to find them. For a few moments, at least.'

'Where were the keys?' Mason said.

'Where Mr Tate left them when he showed us the flat. On a ledge near the door.'

'Mr Tate?' Lyall said.

'Yes, the agent from ATN Property Management. The company who leased us the flat.'

'You're sure that's where they were?'

'Very sure,' Joscowski replied. 'Then the door unlocked and we heard him run down the stairs.'

'Going back to when he was in the house, Ania,' Mason said. 'You told Sergeant Lindsay he was wearing a mask. Did you notice anything else in the brief time you saw him?'

Joscowski shook her head. 'It was really quite dark. I saw the mask for only a moment – when he was close to my face. When he fell back, I got up and ran. I didn't look at him afterwards.'

Lyall closed the notebook, put it in her handbag, and took out a card, which she handed to Ania. 'Okay, thank you both,' she said, then added, 'Ania, this card has my number and details of our rape trauma counselling service. If you remember anything else or need to talk to someone, please give us a ring.'

'This man,' Ania said, 'you know who he is?'

'Not yet, I'm afraid,' Lyall replied.

'But he's attacked before? Raped other women?'

'Yes, Ania. He has.'

'Then you will catch him?'

Lyall smiled reassuringly. 'We're confident we will.'

Ania gave her an earnest look. 'I saw something in his eyes,' she said. 'You know, he was quite willing to use the knife. And if you don't find him, I think he will.'

* * *

'Bit of a coincidence,' Mason said when she and Lyall were back in their car.

'What is?'

'The Tate guy and ATN Property Management.' She paused. 'You know Jack and I are getting married in December?'

'I do, yes,' Lyall said.

'Well, I'm letting my flat and moving into his place. I rang ATN yesterday and Tate called at lunchtime. Took some notes and a few pictures on his iPhone. He must've come straight to my place after the girls signed the lease.'

'A coincidence indeed,' Lyall agreed. 'You know what's equally odd?'

'What?'

'That Ania was attacked so soon after moving in.'

'I agree,' Mason said. 'But there's something stranger still.'

'Go on.'

'He views women as targets of opportunity, right?'

'Right.'

'He comes into the bedroom, sees Lidka, yet bypasses her to get to Ania. Appears to know exactly where her bedroom's located.'

'He has it planned?'

'I think it's highly likely.'

'Hmm,' Lyall said. 'I think we'd better have a word with this Tate guy.'

Chapter Fifteen

'The Wylie brothers weren't the only charlatans,' Arthur Lawson was saying. 'Tuffnell was a bit of a crook, too.'

He, Knox and Fulton were seated in DD Enterprises' office in York Place, a short drive from Gayfield Square Police Station. Lawson had agreed to the interview after Knox had phoned an hour earlier and asked to speak to him about Tuffnell's murder.

'Really?' Knox replied. 'What makes you say that?'

'He knew large sections of *Armageddon 2* had been cloned from *Generation 2042*, the game brought to market by the American company, ETL International, but said nothing. He'd made a packet from their earlier game, *Lancer*, and was quite prepared to look the other way. He knew NewTech's game wasn't kosher.'

'And you discovered this how, sir?'

Lawson was tall and thin and dressed only in a T-shirt and jeans. He studied Knox for a long moment, then said, 'From Tom Baxter, a trade journalist friend of mine who interviewed Tuffnell just before *Armageddon 2's* release.

'During the interview Baxter talked about him handling the share offer and asked about rumours circulating of similarities between the games. Tuffnell insisted there was none. But after the interview concluded and they'd had a few drinks, Tuffnell winked at him and said, "You know as well as I do, Tom, nothing's ever completely original." At which point Tuffnell quickly added, "And that, by the way, is off the record." I've only Baxter's word, of course, but I've known him a long time and have no reason to disbelieve him.'

'Edward Denison told us you have an interest in a company called TayImage?' Knox said.

Lawson nodded. 'Yes, I'm one of the directors.'

'Do you also have an interest in a company called ADL studios?'

Lawson smiled. 'Ah, now I see,' he said. '*Hired Guns*, another game the Wylies plagiarised. Yes, I have an eighth share in the company. We lost a considerable chunk of income as a result of NewTech's rip-off. However, Niles Barnard, one of my ADL colleagues, decided against prosecution because he was a good friend of Wylie senior. But no doubt Edward told you that?'

'Yes, sir, he did.'

'So, Inspector,' Lawson said. 'The reason for your questioning. Was I angry? Yes, very much. But angry enough to commit murder? Definitely not.'

'Did you ever meet Tuffnell?'

'No. But I did see him once, at the Golden Lion pub in Dundee. Edward Denison pointed him out to me. Curiously enough, we were discussing NewTech when the Wylies and Tuffnell came into the bar. I'd seen the brothers at games conventions, of course, but didn't know them personally.'

'And Tuffnell?'

'Like I say, first and only time I saw him,' Lawson said. 'With the Wylies. Edward and I didn't acknowledge them, nor they us.'

'And your meeting with Mr Denison, it concerned his father's investment?'

'Yes. I mentioned the ADL infringement, rumours about cloning *Generation 2042,* and told him to advise his father accordingly. I knew it was only a matter of time before the Yanks discovered their game had been ripped off.'

'Do you happen to know how the Americans found out?'

Lawson shook his head. 'It wasn't me, if that's what you're thinking. What I can tell you is that in this business the grapevine works at warp speed. Wouldn't have taken long for them to get wind.'

Knox dipped his head in acknowledgement. 'Okay,' he said. 'That leaves one final question.'

'Where was I on Monday night?'

'Yes, sir,' Knox said. 'If you don't mind.'

'That's easy,' Lawson replied. 'Malaga. Ten-day break – first to eleventh of September. My BA flight arrived back in Edinburgh at ten-thirty last night.'

* * *

'The field's narrowing a bit,' Fulton said when he and Knox got back in the car. 'Coutts, the Denisons and Lawson – each one with a solid alibi.'

Knox pursed his lips and placed his iPhone on the dash bracket. 'Which leaves us with Mainwaring and Fairborough.' He keyed a number and a few moments later they heard Hathaway's voice on the speakers. 'Boss?'

'The head concierge at the Balmoral, Mark. He's got back to you yet?'

'Yes, boss. A little over half an hour ago.'

'And?'

'Another one indulging in a wee bit of flannel,' Hathaway said. 'Mainwaring lied. Left the hotel and flagged down a taxi at 11.53pm on Monday. Arrived back in his room at 12.23am. The door keys are computerised. Makes a record each time the room is accessed. For security reasons, I guess.'

'How do you know he hailed a cab?'

'There's CCTV at Register House, opposite. After picking up, his taxi does a U-turn and turns right onto North Bridge. The recording shows it turning left again at the junction of North Bridge and High Street.'

'Heading towards Netherbow?'

'Yes,' Hathaway replied. 'Remember the cameras at the corner of St Mary's Street and Canongate I told you about on Tuesday?'

'Yes, go on,' Knox said.

'Well, I got the clothes shop to send me an MP4 file covering the period from 11pm until 12.30am. The images are okay, apart from a corrupted section between 11.41pm and 12.01am, which affects both cameras.'

'What do you mean, corrupted?'

'The shop manager explained there's a short in the cameras' wiring. Apparently they're going to have it fixed, but the technician's been up to his eyes during the Festival. Hasn't got around to it yet.'

'Does it show anything?'

'Two things,' Hathaway said. 'A man with a Jack Russell on a leash in St Mary's Street. Heading towards the foot of the Pleasance. I guess that'll be Mr Everett walking his dog.'

'What time is this?'

'11.33pm.'

'Checks with what he told us,' Knox said. 'Then?'

'Little of interest from either viewpoint from then until 11.41, when the file blanks. The static clears and images pick up again at 12.01. Still not much happening on the camera covering St. Mary's Street, but the one trained on Netherbow shows Mainwaring leaving World's End Close at 12.13am. A moment later he hails a cab and heads back to the hotel.'

'And that's all that can be seen at the close entrance?' Knox said. 'Mainwaring appearing at 12.13am and flagging down a taxi?'

'Aye, boss,' Hathaway replied. 'He exits the close, waves, and the taxi stops.'

'How good is the definition?'

'I was able to zoom in reasonably close, but it's pretty grainy.'

'Can you tell if he looks dishevelled?'

'The section showing him leaving and getting into the cab lasts only 11.2 seconds. Looks like he's wearing a suit and tie, but there isn't much clarity.'

'Okay,' Knox said. 'We've enough to arrest him. Get in touch with Stirling police and have him brought in.'

'Righto, boss. What's the charge, if they ask?'

'Obstructing the course of justice for now. We'll see if that changes after we talk to him.'

* * *

Myra was at the reception and Turnbull in his office when Tate arrived. He went to his desk, switched on his desktop computer and checked his e-mails, but his inbox was empty.

He glanced at Myra. 'Any viewings scheduled?' he asked.

'None,' she replied and indicated the phone. 'Only one call this morning from the contract plumber. Told us he finished fitting a new bathroom suite at a property in Raeburn Place on Tuesday.' She glanced towards their boss's door. 'I don't know why Mr Turnbull bothered. The plasterers aren't due to start there for a fortnight.'

Tate nodded and opened his copy of the *Daily Record*. Too early yet for a mention of an attempted assault at Viewforth Square. No doubt that would be covered in the *Evening News,* which came out later that morning.

He cast his mind back over events, gave an involuntary shake of the head, and winced. When he'd examined himself in the bathroom mirror that morning he'd seen a thick, three-inch black and blue welt just above his shoulder. His neck ached like hell every time he moved, and he put on a turtleneck sweater to cover it.

He realised there was a likelihood police might call at the office. He'd racked his brains on the way there, examining possible scenarios. He'd tried to make it look like it had been a random intruder, and thought he'd been successful. But was there anything that might give him away?

He didn't think so. He'd entered by the window, unlatching the lock from the outside. What's more, he'd taken the precaution of wearing gloves, so there wouldn't be fingerprints or DNA.

What else?

He'd had his mask on throughout, so the bitch couldn't have seen his face. Nowak had locked the pair of them in her room, while he was searching for the front door keys.

The keys.

They'd been on a ledge behind the door and the lights had been off. He knew they were likely to be there because that's where he'd left them on Wednesday, when he showed the women the flat. But a stranger mightn't have found them so easily, particularly in darkness.

Or would he? There was light in the hallway. Not much, but some. The living room door had been slightly ajar, and street lighting afforded a glimmer of illumination.

He'd read somewhere that in low light the iris widens and dilates the pupils, enhancing eyesight. It was likely an intruder would have spotted the keys.

No, he didn't think he'd anything to fear there.

His reverie was interrupted when the door opened and two women entered. He recognised one immediately – Mason, the cop he'd visited at Warrender Park Terrace.

Both women were dressed in suits, so it was safe to assume – as he'd guessed earlier – that they'd called in connection with Joscowski's assault.

Myra looked up and was about say something, but Mason ignored her and smiled at him. 'Mr Tate, isn't it?'

she said. 'You called at my place yesterday, to discuss a lease?'

'Yes,' Tate said, then nodded to the office. 'Did you want to talk it over with my boss?'

'No, thanks – official visit, I'm afraid.' She waved to her colleague. 'This is DS Lyall. We're here to discuss two of your clients. Ms Nowak and Ms Joscowski. They signed an agreement with you yesterday on a flat in Viewforth Square?'

Turnbull exited his office at that moment and gave the detectives a concerned look. 'Good morning,' he said. 'I overheard what you said to Derek about the Polish girls. Was there a problem?'

'I'm sorry,' Lyall said. 'You are?'

'George Turnbull,' he replied. 'Proprietor of ATN Property Management.'

'Good morning, Mr Turnbull,' Lyall said, showing him her warrant card. 'I'm DS Lyall and my colleague is DC Mason. We were asking Mr Tate about an agreement with Ms Nowak and Ms Joscowski on a flat in Viewforth Square.'

'Yes,' Turnbull said. 'He showed the girls the flat and they signed a six-month lease. Why do you ask?'

'Because a man broke into the flat last night. Ms Joscowski was subjected to attempted rape.'

Turnbull paled visibly. 'Oh, my God,' he said.

'We thought Mr Tate might be able to help us. The women were given to understand he carried out an inspection of the property before they moved in?'

'Yes,' Turnbull replied. 'Of course, he did. We pre-inspect all the properties on our books. How did the intruder gain access?'

'Via a faulty catch on the rear bedroom window.'

'Really?' Turnbull said, then turned towards Tate. 'You checked it on Tuesday, didn't you, Derek?'

'Yes, Mr Turnbull,' Tate said. 'I didn't see anything amiss.'

'It would help if we could speak to you a minute, Mr Tate,' Lyall said. 'To discover if you were aware of anything out of the ordinary. You wouldn't mind?'

'No, of course not,' Tate replied.

Lyall waved towards the back of the premises, and addressed Turnbull. 'Could we use your office, sir?'

'Yes,' he replied. 'Please, go ahead.'

Chapter Sixteen

'I told you I'd been at the hotelier's meeting at the Balmoral,' Mainwaring was saying. 'And that was true.'

He and his solicitor Magnus Stuart were sitting opposite Knox and Fulton in an interview room shortly after he'd been taken to Gayfield Square and charged with obstruction.

'It was also true that I went to my room just after eleven,' Mainwaring added.

'But you left again shortly afterwards?' Knox said.

'Yes. May I explain why?'

'Carry on.'

'As I told you yesterday, we had a drink afterwards. One of the attendees was a man called Ron Wilson, a director with Excelsior Cruises, a company based in London. Anyway, we began chatting. I mentioned my mother's investment in the games industry, her loss when NewTech went bankrupt, and the subsequent case against Tuffnell.

'Wilson asked if Tuffnell worked with Fairborough and Noble. I said he did, then he told me Tuffnell was staying at the Travelodge in St Mary's Street. Wilson stayed there too when he was in the city and they were on a nodding acquaintance. He'd seen Tuffnell book in that morning.

'When I got back to my room I began thinking about how Tuffnell's duplicity had cost us a fortune. More, it had resulted in Mr Denison's suicide and very likely contributed to my mother's stroke. The longer I mulled it over, the more angry I became. I decided to go to the Travelodge and confront Tuffnell. Make him admit he'd known about the Wylies' fakery all along.'

'But you'd lost your case in court,' Knox said. 'What made you think he'd admit it?'

'I didn't,' Mainwaring said. 'I just wanted to call him a liar – to his face.'

'Okay,' Knox said. 'So you left the hotel and got into a taxi. What happened then?'

'The High Street was busy. Pubs emptying, a fair number of tourists about. The driver slowed on approach to Netherbow, where there was a line of traffic. The lights changed to red and we stopped.'

'Where was the taxi then?' Knox asked.

'Almost opposite the Museum of Childhood.'

'Just up from Netherbow?' Fulton asked.

'Yes,' Mainwaring replied. 'Suddenly Tuffnell stepped from the pavement and crossed in front of us, heading back to his hotel. He was wavering a bit, so I wasn't the only one who'd been drinking. I paid the cabbie, got out of the taxi and followed. I caught up with him outside World's End Close.'

'Go on,' Knox said.

'I tapped him on the shoulder and said, "Adrian Tuffnell?"

'He stopped and glared at me. "Who are you?" he said.

'"Richard Mainwaring," I replied. "You may remember I accompanied my mother back in April, when Edward Denison brought a court case against you."

'He looked at me for several seconds, then said, "Oh, I remember now, you're one of the investors who claimed

I'd prior knowledge of NewTech's theft of intellectual property."

"'I am,' I said. "You told Denison you'd seen both games, and that NewTech's bore no resemblance to the American one."

"'Did I?' he said. "Then why was the case thrown out? The fact is I'd said no such thing. And Denison had no proof that I had."

"'Which was what you played on, wasn't it?' I said. "That there was nothing in writing. Your cut was substantial, and you were prepared to do anything to protect it, including lying."

"'You accuse me of greed,' he said. "Yet all three investors – your mother included – knew the risks involved. They were stock-exchange veterans who'd profited handsomely over the years. Don't forget they'd signed a contract where the small print reads: 'share prices, their value and the income from them can go down as well as up, and investors may get back less than their original investment.'"

'At this point, I lost my rag. "But it wasn't an *investment*, was it?" I said. "My mother and the others unknowingly backed a rip-off. What's more, you knew if it backfired – correction, *when* it backfired – their loss was certain. The only thing you cared about was your fucking commission."

"'That's business, son,' he sneered. "Live with it."

'I gave him a shove, and he staggered back into the close. "What about my mother?" I said. "She suffered a stroke from the stress. That's something she has to *live* with? And the Denisons, their father committed suicide after losing his life savings. They've to live with that, too?"

'Tuffnell shrugged. "Nothing I intend losing sleep over," he said. "Now bugger off, out of my way."

'He made to walk past me, but my blood was up. I threw a right-hander which caught his jaw, and he dropped to the ground. I think his head hit the floor, as he appeared unconscious. I stood until my temper subsided, and decided to call it a day. I walked back to the High Street and flagged down a taxi.'

'How far into the close were you?' Knox asked.

'Not that far. A few feet, maybe.'

'You hadn't gone to the courtyard at the back?'

'No.'

'Tuffnell was found with multiple head wounds near communal rubbish bins. You didn't carry the fight to the end of the close, pick up a brick and hit him with it?'

'My client has stated he went a short distance into the entrance,' Stuart said, raising a hand in objection. 'And delivered a single blow with his fist.'

Knox acknowledged Stuart with a glance, then studied Mainwaring for a long moment. 'What time did you hail the taxi?' he asked.

Mainwaring shook his head. 'I'm not sure. Just after midnight, I think.'

'Were you wearing gloves?'

'*What?*'

'It's a simple question,' Knox said. 'Were you wearing gloves?'

Mainwaring gave Knox a querulous look. 'No,' he said. 'Why the hell would I wear gloves?'

Knox ignored the question. 'As I stated a moment ago, Adrian Tuffnell was found in the courtyard with multiple head injuries. You've admitted to being in the close and throwing a punch which rendered him unconscious.' Knox nodded to the NEAL recording machine, and added, 'You also admitted, quote, that, "Your blood was up". You expect us to believe you didn't carry it further?'

'I really must object to this line of questioning,' Stuart said. 'My client already told you–'

'No, it's okay,' Mainwaring interrupted. 'I'll give him his answer, and ask a question of my own. Was I angry? Yes. Did I thump him and knock him unconscious? Again, yes. Now, Inspector, my question: you mentioned a brick and multiple head wounds. If I'd carried on and murdered

Tuffnell as you suggest, my DNA would be on the murder weapon, would it not?' He paused for effect. 'So, why not subject me to a test?'

Knox studied Mainwaring for a long moment. 'We will, sir. But in the meantime I have to tell you that you're being remanded on suspicion of murder.'

Stuart glanced at his watch. 'You arrested my client at 11.47am this morning. You're aware you can only hold him until the same time tomorrow if a DNA test proves negative?'

Knox nodded to a uniformed officer who came forward and placed a hand on Mainwaring's shoulder. 'I am, Mr Stuart,' he said. 'Very aware.'

* * *

'You think Mainwaring's guilty?' Fulton asked Knox when they were back in the office.

'I'm not sure,' Knox replied. 'He seemed confident his DNA would be absent on the brick used to bludgeon Tuffnell.'

'Mr Murray said no recent DNA was found on the murder weapon. Only nitrile glove residue.'

'Which would make Mainwaring's DNA test seem pointless,' Knox said.

'But you're going to take one anyway?'

'Yes,' Knox replied, 'The forensics results on Tuffnell's clothes aren't in yet. You never know what they might find.'

Hathaway looked up from his desktop computer and addressed Knox. 'You might want to see this, boss,' he said.

Knox and Fulton went to his desk, where Hathaway indicated the monitor. 'After I checked the clothes shop file, I got to wondering where Tuffnell had been before making his way back to St Mary's Street.'

'And?' Knox said.

'I found this, from the CCTV camera of a bank at the corner of Cockburn Street and High Street. It's directly linked to our system.'

Fulton took out a pair of reading glasses, put them on, and peered closer. 'That's the Filling Station restaurant and bar, almost opposite St Giles.'

'It is,' Hathaway agreed. 'I've stopped the recording at 11.49pm. Wait till I forward it a bit.' He touched his finger to the mouse and the counter advanced to 11.52pm. 'There,' he added. 'Isn't that Tuffnell?'

The screenshot showed two men, both in their early sixties, one more rotund and shorter than the other. 'Aye,' Fulton said. 'And the other guy's Fairborough.'

Knox shook his head and gave a grunt of cynicism. 'Fairborough – who told us he hadn't seen Tuffnell since Wednesday 4 September.'

'And claimed they seldom socialised,' Fulton added.

'Uh-huh,' Knox said. 'We'll have to have another word.' He gestured to the desktop monitor, and added, 'Okay, Mark. Let's see the rest.'

Hathaway clicked and the video began to spool forward, showing Fairborough and Tuffnell in animated conversation for a further two minutes, when a cab came to a halt at the edge of the pavement. Fairborough shook Tuffnell's hand and entered the taxi, which drove off.

Hathaway manipulated the mouse and the video zoomed out. He indicated the screen and said, 'As you can see, the taxi turns into Cockburn Street. I checked with the cab company, Central Radio Taxis. They dropped Fairborough in Heriot Row at three minutes after midnight.' He adjusted the picture and the camera re-focussed on the second man. 'Tuffnell continues on his way down the High Street to the North Bridge junction, where he exits the camera's field of view.'

Knox glanced at the time counter at the corner of the video pane. 'And is out of shot at 11.56pm. Three minutes after Mainwaring boarded his cab outside the Balmoral.'

He considered this for a moment. 'Yes, that fits, they would have crossed paths when Mainwaring said they did.' Knox's phone rang at that moment and he keyed the *accept* icon and said, 'Ed?'

'Afternoon, Jack,' the forensics officer replied. 'Howdenhall just completed their tests on Tuffnell's clothes.'

'Anything interesting?'

'No DNA, I'm afraid. However, Alex Turley's idea that some kind of ligature was put around his neck is spot on. Fragments of gravel and other material were found on the back of his jacket and trouser legs. Consistent with him being dragged from the close to the rubbish bins where he was found.'

'But nothing else?'

'Afraid not. The only other results were from Liz Beattie's forensics on the window of the flat at Viewforth Square.'

'The attempted rape of the Polish girl?'

'Yes. No DNA found there either, unfortunately. Though there are signs that indicate the lock might have been tampered with. Liz has forwarded details to DS Lyall and Mason. They're talking to the property agent now.'

Chapter Seventeen

'I gave the flat a complete inspection prior to the Polish girls moving in,' Tate was saying. Turnbull had shown the detectives into his office, pulled extra chairs to his desk, and left them to their interview.

'We always do this prior to tenants moving in,' Tate continued. 'Sometimes a property has lain empty for weeks. We've to make sure everything is in order. You know, gas and electricity turned on, telephone service in place, that sort of thing.'

Lyall's iPhone beeped and she glanced at the message for a few moments, then addressed Tate. 'You checked the window catch in Ms Nowak's room,' she said. 'It didn't appear damaged in any way?'

'No.' Tate shrugged and added, 'We're responsible only for leasing the properties and a certain amount of maintenance. Any upgrades vis-à-vis security is in the hands of the owners. When properties haven't been upgraded, the rental is often lower, as is the case here.'

Lyall glanced at her phone again. 'How closely did you examine the catch on Ms Nowak's bedroom window?'

Tate gave her a diffident look. 'I've already said, it appeared okay.'

'One of our forensic officers just completed an examination. Her report reveals there are scratches consistent with tampering.'

'But that's how the intruder accessed the flat,' Tate said. 'He must've used something.'

'No, you misunderstand,' Lyall said. 'These scratches are on the *inside*.' She glanced at her phone again, and added, 'To quote my colleague, "A screwdriver or similar tool has been used to slacken the catch lever from above the sash bar, leaving several small marks on the paintwork."'

Tate shook his head. 'Sorry, I missed that,' he said. 'I seem to recall the previous tenants were male students. They must have been responsible.'

Mason gave an acknowledging nod, and changed tack. 'When you showed Ms Joscowski and Ms Nowak the flat, did either express preference for a particular room?'

'Yes,' Tate replied. 'Ms Nowak said she didn't sleep well, she was concerned that traffic noise at the front might keep her awake. She asked Ms Joscowski if she'd mind if she took the back bedroom. Ms Joscowski agreed.'

'You see, Derek,' Mason said. 'We were wondering about the attacker's behaviour. Why, with no prior knowledge of the property, did he bypass Ms Nowak to go to Ms Joscowski's room?'

A bead of sweat formed on Tate's left temple, moments later breaking into a rivulet, which ran down his cheek. He shrugged. 'I dunno, maybe someone saw them move in. Ms Joscowski might have someone who's stalking her. When he saw Nowak, he realised she must be in another room.'

'Possible,' Lyall said. 'But there's another thing that's strange.'

'What?' Tate said.

'The keys. The flat was in semi-darkness the entire time. The girls locked themselves in Ms Nowak's room, cutting off his exit route. Yet he knew exactly where to find them – on a ledge near the door. How do you suppose that was?'

Tate appeared flustered. 'It's – it's not that unusual,' he said. 'In many flats I see, owners or tenants leave their keys near the door, either on a ledge or a hook.'

'Not in their handbag or coat pocket?' Mason said. 'That's where I keep mine.'

'Some folk are different, I suppose,' Tate said, regaining some of his composure. 'No. Many leave them just where I did yesterday. If your intruder's in the habit of breaking into properties, he'll probably know to check there, too.'

The detectives said nothing for a long moment, then Mason asked, 'Where were you at 9.20pm on Monday, Derek?'

Tate's face registered annoyance. 'You honestly think I had anything to do with the assault they're reporting in the papers? And the attack on Ms Joscowski?'

'We think the individual who raped a girl in the Meadows on Monday is the same man who attacked Ania last night. Your build and height is similar to the attacker's profile.'

'And there are several factors present which make it important that we rule you out, Mr Tate,' Lyall added. 'You knew about the window; had knowledge of the layout of the property and where the girls were sleeping; and were aware of the exact location of the house keys.'

'But I've explained all that,' Tate said.

'I know, Derek,' Mason said. 'You do understand, though, why circumstances make you a suspect?'

Tate studied Mason for a long moment, then shrugged. '9.20pm on Monday?' he said. 'I was at home, 23 Kilmaurs Grove. I live with my parents.' He took a slim book from the inside pocket of his jacket, handed it to Mason, and continued, 'Check my appointments diary. I'd been showing a flat in Howe Street to a couple in the process of moving to Edinburgh from Leeds. They signed the lease, I gave them the keys, and drove home.'

'What time did you leave Howe Street?' Mason asked.

'Just after eight. I got back half an hour later.'

Mason leafed through the diary and found the page for Monday 9 September, where a pencilled entry read: "7.30pm. Mr & Mrs Carter, 129 Howe Street."

'You understand we'll have to contact your parents for corroboration?' Mason said.

'Of course.'

Lyall opened her handbag, took out an envelope, then donned a pair of nitrile gloves and removed a small tube. 'This is a DNA specimen kit, Mr Tate,' she said. 'It contains an oral swab, which is used to take a saliva sample from inside your cheek. You've no objection?'

Tate felt panic rise in his throat, which he managed to suppress. 'No,' he said.

* * *

'Did I really tell you I hadn't seen Adrian since a week past Wednesday?' Fairborough was saying. Knox and Fulton had returned to Charlotte Square later that afternoon and the three men were in his office.

Knox glanced at his notebook. 'Yes, sir. Those words exactly.'

'I'm sorry,' Fairborough said. 'I must've been confused. We've been particularly busy this past week or so.'

'As we discussed, you were at the Filling Station with Mr Tuffnell on Monday evening, and left at 11.50pm. Could you tell me what it was that couldn't wait until your scheduled meeting on Tuesday?'

'Nothing. Adrian invited me for a meal and a drink. I accepted.'

'Did he have anything in particular he wanted to discuss?'

'Not really. We speculated on which shares were likely to rise, which were likely to fall. That sort of thing.'

'You didn't discuss the NewTech deal?'

'No. Why?'

'Because differences have arisen between what you said and what the NewTech investors told us.'

'Really?' Fairborough said.

'Yes,' Knox said. 'For example, you told us you didn't deal directly with any of Mr Tuffnell's clients. That wasn't true, was it?'

'You're talking about Frances Mainwaring?'

'I am.'

'Mrs Mainwaring didn't care for Mr Tuffnell, she nominated me to handle the trade.'

'But you told us he dealt with NewTech's business for all three clients.'

Fairborough cleared his throat. 'Which was true. Adrian took care of the NewTech share sale.'

'Including Mrs Mainwaring's investment?'

'Yes, he'd been instrumental in NewTech going public. He insisted on handling the transaction.'

'Do you think Mrs Mainwaring might have gone ahead if she knew her shares were being managed by Tuffnell?' Knox said.

Fairborough made an open-handed gesture. 'Perhaps. The effect was the same.'

'It wasn't, though, was it?' Knox said. 'She lost her investment.'

'In the event, yes. I wasn't to know that at the time.'

'Did you not?' Knox said. 'After Edward Denison discovered the breach of copyright, Mrs Mainwaring rang you. She claims you told her you supported what Tuffnell told Edward Denison – the intellectual property of *Armageddon 2* was the Wylies'.'

'I did speak to Adrian after Denison called Richard. He assured me there were no similarities between the games.'

'Yet when the investors asked you to repeat that in court, you refused to appear. Why?'

'Because, like the investors, I'd only Adrian's word. I couldn't prove what he'd said. To have gone would have been pointless.'

Knox shook his head. 'Mrs Mainwaring and the others' losses didn't really affect you, did they?'

'What do you mean?'

'I think it's obvious,' Knox said. 'The NewTech debacle cost you three large accounts – Mrs Mainwaring, the Denisons and Brigadier Coutts all tell me they've taken their business elsewhere. Yet you were still meeting the man who lost those accounts. Tuffnell remained contracted to your company, and you were seeing him socially. With what the two of you earned in commissions, you came out of the deal rather well.'

Knox nodded to Fulton and the detectives stood. 'As you know, I'm in the middle of a murder inquiry,' he added. 'And it's not my department. But I think you and Tuffnell knew about the Wylies' deception, which you aided and abetted. I'll be forwarding details to our Financial Frauds Office for investigation.'

Fairborough's face turned beetroot-red. 'Damn you, man,' he sputtered. 'I know the Chief Constable. I intend to complain about that allegation.'

'If you think it'll help, sir,' Knox replied, 'I advise you to go ahead.'

* * *

'So, you think Tate's our rapist?' Knox was asking Lyall. They and the three other members of the team had gathered in the office later that afternoon and were discussing progress.

'Ninety-nine per cent sure, boss,' Lyall replied. 'Yvonne and I studied the George IV Bridge bank recording again and there's a match, both in height and physicality.'

'His demeanour during our interview at ATN Property Management's offices made us suspicious,' Mason said. 'He was sweating, fidgeting, unable to maintain eye contact. More importantly, he knew the layout of the flat and where both girls were sleeping. We think he intended Ania Joscowski to take the back bedroom and had to change plans at the last minute because her flatmate was a light sleeper.'

'The women told you about their sleeping arrangements?' Knox said.

'No, boss. Tate did.'

'Liz Beattie carried out an examination of the window catch,' Lyall said. 'It was tampered with from the inside – she photographed tiny scratch marks on the paint with a close-up lens. We think Tate loosened it to make it easier to spring the catch from the other side.'

'We're guessing the original plan was to exit the way he entered,' Mason added. 'But, when Ania retreated to the other bedroom and the girls locked themselves in, he was forced to leave by the front door.'

'The keys, too, are a bit of a giveaway,' Lyall said. 'The flat was in semi-darkness, yet the intruder managed to locate them on a ledge in seconds. The same ledge where Tate left them when he signed over the flat to the girls.'

Knox dipped his head in acknowledgement. 'Did Liz find anything else?'

'No fingerprints,' Mason said. 'And she doesn't think there's DNA evidence, either – looks like he was wearing gloves.'

'But you swabbed him?'

'Yes,' Lyall said. 'The Howdenhall courier picked up his sample an hour ago. We've marked it urgent and phoned Liz. She's promised to prioritise the analysis and let us have the results tomorrow morning.'

'Has he an alibi for Monday evening?'

Lyall nodded. 'He lives with his parents at Kilmaurs Grove. Says he was home from 8.30pm onwards. We'll talk to them tomorrow, but we're hoping that'll come after his arrest, when we get the results from Howdenhall.'

Knox gave a hint of a smile. 'You're that confident?'

'Yes, boss,' Lyall and Mason chorused.

'Excellent,' Knox said, then turned and saw the DCI exit his office and walk towards him.

'Kate and Yvonne have updated you on their suspicions about Tate, the property rental rep?' Warburton asked.

'Yes, sir,' Knox replied. 'If the DNA result proves positive, we'll pick him up in the morning.'

Warburton nodded. 'And Richard Mainwaring?'

'We've sent a specimen of his DNA up to Howdenhall, too. As you know, he's been remanded in custody.'

'You think it could be him? Even though forensics found no DNA on the murder weapon?'

'He was at the scene and admits to assaulting Tuffnell.'

'But that took place a short distance into the close? We've no proof he actually dragged Tuffnell to where he was found?'

'I know, sir. I was hoping for something from his suit. Unfortunately, the results proved negative.'

'So, what next?'

'I've a hunch there's something else. I'd like to have another word before I release him.'

'Okay, Jack. But don't hold him longer than necessary. Magnus Stuart, his solicitor, has been breathing down my neck all afternoon.'

Chapter Eighteen

The moment the detectives left the premises, Tate gave a protracted sigh of relief. When the older cop had taken his DNA, he'd been convinced they were about to arrest him. Then it dawned that the specimen would have to be submitted for analysis before they obtained a result.

How long might that take? A day? Two days? It didn't matter, the game was up. As soon as they ran the test, a match would be found with the women he'd had sex with. At which point they'd be back to arrest him.

Except that it wouldn't happen. He'd made contingency plans, and now was the time to put them into practice.

He re-entered the front office and Turnbull gave him a sympathetic look. 'Don't worry, Derek,' he said. 'Police procedure. Damn bad luck an intruder should have struck the very night the women took up their tenancy. Casts us all in a bad light, eh? But there's no doubt in my mind that you gave the property a thorough check, so don't blame yourself.

'I remember seeing the flat when we took it on three years ago. I told the owner then he should upgrade: fit double-glazed windows with modern security locks, as most of his neighbours had done. Particularly with a fire escape just outside.' Turnbull shrugged. 'Just asking for trouble.

'The detectives,' he continued, 'they were happy with what you told them?'

Tate wasn't about to disclose what questions he'd been asked or that DNA had been taken. 'As you say, Mr Turnbull,' he replied. 'Fairly routine stuff: they were curious if I'd noticed anything when I checked the window, had the back door been unlocked… that sort of thing.'

Content with this explanation, Turnbull had returned to his office, reappearing at 12.30pm, when he said, 'Myra, I'm having lunch with a chap who's purchased a new-build block of flats in Leith. If anyone calls, tell them to ring back this afternoon.' Then to Tate, 'No viewings scheduled, Derek, but if anything comes in, you'll take care of it?'

'Of course, Mr Turnbull.'

After Turnbull departed, Tate stood and nodded to his office. 'Just realised I left my appointments book on the boss's desk when I spoke to the detectives this morning. I'll go and get it.'

Myra looked up distractedly from the magazine she was reading. 'Eh?' she said, then added, 'Oh. Right, Derek.'

He went to a filing cabinet behind Turnbull's desk and opened it. In the corner at the back was a biscuit tin, inside which was a duplicate key of every property on ATN's books, each identified with a small handwritten label looped through the key with an elastic band.

A master copy of every key was kept in readiness in a glass cabinet in the front office, but Tate knew Turnbull liked to keep back-ups for security. In the event, his boss had never needed these duplicates, and they were seldom checked.

Tate riffled through the tags until he found the one he was looking for: 18a Raeburn Place. The flat Myra had alluded to earlier; the one where a new bathroom suite had been fitted.

He pocketed the key, placed the lid back on the biscuit tin and closed the file drawer, then went back to the front office, where Myra was still engrossed in her magazine.

He nodded to the entrance. 'I'm going to Subway for a couple of rolls and a coffee,' he said. 'Want anything?'

Myra gestured to a plastic container on her desk. 'I've got sandwiches,' she said, reaching for her handbag. 'You can fetch me a coffee, though.'

'Okay,' Tate said, then held up his hand. 'Don't worry about the cash – you can pay me when I get back.'

He left the office and turned into a narrow lane where his Honda Civic was parked. He started the car, turned left into Bruntsfield Place, then right again into Whitehouse Loan. Going back to the office was the last thing on his mind. No, he was headed to Kilmaurs Grove, to pick up what he needed before going into hiding.

He had a story ready, one which he hoped would steer the cops in the wrong direction. It had been quiet at the office, he'd tell his parents, and his boss had given him a couple of days off to coincide with the weekend. His parents knew him to be a keen photographer, and he'd tell them he was off to Skye for a short camping break, where he hoped to capture some interesting sunsets over the Quiraing.

The fact was, he'd planned quite a different destination entirely…

* * *

'I'm satisfied you left World's End Close when you said you did,' Knox was saying. He and Fulton were back in the interview room with Richard Mainwaring and his solicitor Magnus Stuart.

'We don't yet have the results of your DNA test,' Knox continued, 'but other forensic evidence and CCTV images leads us to believe you were innocent of the murder of Mr Tuffnell.'

'So my client is free to go?' Stuart asked.

'Yes,' Knox said. 'However, before you do, Mr Mainwaring, I'd be grateful if you answer a couple of questions.'

'Of course,' Mainwaring said, his relief at being released apparent. 'Anything I can do to help.'

'Firstly, I'd like to say that we spoke again to Mr Fairborough, and I believe both he and Tuffnell knew that the Wylie brothers had cloned elements of the American game. A fact he deliberately hid from your mother and the other investors.

'I know it's little comfort in view of your mother's health and financial losses, but I've asked our Financial Frauds division to investigate.'

Mainwaring dipped his head in acknowledgement. 'Thank you, Inspector, I appreciate that, and I'm sure my mother will, too.' He paused. 'Now, what was it you wanted to ask me?'

'It's to help our frauds people, really,' Knox said. 'When I spoke to your mother, she told me Fairborough was handling her investment, is that true?'

'Yes.'

'Could you let me know what amount was involved, sir?'

'£675,000, which included a tranche of £50,000 which my mother was investing for a third party.'

'A third party?'

'Yes, her chauffeur was retiring. Some time before he'd asked my mother if she would recommend a stock which was likely to rise and provide income for him in his old age. After giving it some thought, she recommended NewTech. He invested his life savings – £50,000.'

'Which he lost when the company was bankrupted?'

'Yes. I think Mother was more devastated over his loss than her own. She felt responsible, having recommended the stock. She insisted he accept compensation of £10,000, which she paid from her own diminished capital.'

'This chauffeur, sir, you said he retired?'

'Yes. Back in May, I think.'

'Do you happen to know his name?'

'Only his Christian name… James. Mother always called him Jimmy, though. I seem to recall her telling me he lives in the Old Town – the Cowgate, Blackfriars Street, somewhere like that.'

'Could you find out his surname for me?'

'Sure,' Mainwaring replied. 'I'll ask Mother when I get back and give you a ring.'

Knox reached inside his jacket and took out a card, which he handed over. 'My mobile number,' he said. 'In case I'm at home when you call.'

* * *

Tate stowed a tent and other camping gear in the boot of the Civic, said goodbye to his parents, and drove the short distance to Esslemont Road. There he parked the car, retrieved a large holdall, and boarded a bus for the city centre. The bus arrived in Raeburn Place thirty minutes later, where he alighted and let himself into 18a.

The flat was empty, save for an old sofa and card table, which the plumbers had used during meal breaks when they'd installed the bathroom suite.

Tate opened the holdall and took out several items. He placed these on the table and began to think. If the cops swallowed the story he'd told his parents, it was likely they'd assume he'd gone to ground in the Highlands, which would give him time to put his plan into action.

Two years ago, before joining ATN, he'd spent the summer at Benidorm in Spain, where he'd sold timeshare properties in an area called Playa de Altea. He'd joined a company owned by Ray King, an East Ender in his thirties who'd grown rich in the burgeoning timeshare market. Tate had proved one of King's star salesmen, successfully persuading hundreds of holidaymakers to realise their dream of two- or four-week guaranteed exclusivity at their own place in the sun.

The problem then, as now, had been sex. Thousands of young females flocked to the area each year and, although Tate had his choice of available young women, he preferred those who weren't too promiscuous – desirable girls in their late teens and twenties who sometimes said no.

Trouble was, Tate wasn't the type to accept such an answer. And, on more than one occasion, this had resulted in his dates crying rape.

The first was a young redhead from Liverpool, who went with him for a meal and a drink to a bar in Cap Negret. Afterwards she accepted his invitation for a nightcap at his flat. Tate poured two tequilas and sat with her on the sofa, then his hands began to wander.

She tried to push him away, but he pinioned her arms and forced himself on her. She left soon afterwards, refusing his offer to pay for a taxi. Next morning he was awoken at eight by two members of the *Guardia Civil*, who took him to a local magistrate. The girl had accused him of rape, the magistrate said, and he'd be remanded in custody until a hearing was arranged.

He was beginning to despair when he heard keys turn in the cell door and the jailer released him. The duty officer said the woman had withdrawn her complaint and he was free to go. Tate left the building and saw King waiting beside his Mercedes.

'The local sergeant tipped me the wink,' he said. 'And I had a word with the girl at her hotel. Told her rape was a difficult charge to prove here in Spain. It would require her to remain in the country for a while. Luckily, she saw sense and dropped the charges.' He tapped the side of his nose and added, 'Mind you, I made clear it was just the sort of story the UK tabloids loved. That might have helped her decision.'

He'd been careful for a while after that, then in late August he met a dark-haired girl from Seville who was in the area with her parents. Her father, a builder called Estrella, was in the process of leasing a block of seafront properties to King in Playa de Altea. Tate and the builder's daughter – whose name was Sofía – were immediately attracted to one another.

On their first date he took her to a restaurant where they had a meal, and at the end of the evening he drove her back to her hotel. They kissed goodnight and arranged to meet the following morning, his day off.

Tate picked her up at nine and they drove to the Sierra Aitana mountains, where Safari Aitana wildlife park was located. They spent the day there, seeing the animals in a natural habitat and taking in the beauty of the location.

On the return journey it was growing dusk when Tate pulled into a secluded layby, where his kissing became impassioned. He activated the reclining passenger seat, pulled up her skirt, and, ignoring her tearful protests, took her virginity.

He tried to apologise afterwards but Sofía said nothing, and when he dropped her at her hotel, she slammed the passenger door and stormed into the lobby.

He shrugged it off, returned to his flat and went to bed, and at 2am was awoken by a banging at the door. He opened it to find King standing with a serious look on his face. 'Shake a leg, son,' he said. 'The *Guardia* is after you.'

'Why?' Tate asked.

'Come on, Derek. I was in the middle of a deal with Estrella. Why'd you have to fuck his daughter? She's screaming rape.'

'I– I'm sorry, Ray.'

'Save it, son,' King said. 'I'll need to put you up until this thing blows over.'

Chapter Twenty

Except it didn't blow over. He spent four days with King, and on the second his protector arrived home at his villa in La Nucia Hills with a worried look on his face.

'It's bad, Derek,' King said. 'Estrella's livid. I told him you'd buggered off but I don't think he believes me. Sergeant Luca tells me he has a helluva lot of influence with the local chief. Apparently, the entire force is looking for you.'

'What can I do, Ray?' Tate said.

'Got a recent photo?'

'What?'

'A recent photo.'

'Of myself? Sorry. No, I haven't.'

'Doesn't matter, I've a camera and we can take one now. There's a lad in Valencia who can fix me up with a passport. Only thing is it'll take a couple of days to get ready. Once we have it, I'll drive you to Madrid and get you on the first flight back to Blighty.' He glanced at Tate, and added, 'You haven't shaved in a few days, which is good. It'll add to your disguise. I've got a pair of thick-rimmed specs somewhere. Change your look entirely.'

'You're sure it's necessary, Ray? I really have to go?'

'Better believe it. Estrella isn't messing about. You've set the cat among the pigeons.' He gave Tate a sympathetic glance, and added, 'Look, son, you're my best salesman and it hurts me to lose you. But the alternative is to see you banged up for ten or fifteen years.'

'It's that serious?'

'Serious as a heart attack,' King said. 'Look, go home; give it a few months. Likely Estrella will be back in Seville by then and it'll blow over. I'll give you a bell when it's safe to return.'

Two days later King handed over the passport and drove him to Madrid-Barajas Airport, where he boarded a flight for Heathrow under the name of Peter Jackson, a refrigeration engineer. He passed through border control in London without a problem and changed flights for Edinburgh.

Soon after arriving in the city he got a job with ATN Property Management and settled back into life at home.

King had been true to his word, however. In March the following year he rang and told Tate that Estrella had returned to Seville and Sergeant Luca, his 'friendly' contact with the local police, had told him the case had been shelved.

King said he was willing to re-hire him and would pay for his flight. Tate thanked him but declined, saying he'd settled into his new life as a leasing representative with ATN.

'Anytime you change your mind, Derek,' King had told him. 'Remember to get in touch. There's a job waiting for you.'

Tate picked up the passport from the card table and flicked it open. If he put on a pair of thick-framed glasses now he'd look much the same as he did then. A couple of days without shaving would see him with a similar amount of stubble. Once again he'd be Peter Jackson, refrigeration engineer. More importantly, if cops were watching the airport, he'd pass without attracting their interest.

* * *

Mason was in the kitchen making coffee and Knox in the bedroom shaving when his landline phone rang. Knox set his electric razor on the dresser and called out, 'I'll get it.'

'Okay,' Mason replied.

Knox padded through to the sitting room and picked up the cordless handset from the charger. 'Knox,' he said.

'Morning, Jack.'

Knox immediately recognised the voice of Ed Murray. 'Morning, Ed,' he said. 'It's the DNA results?'

'Yes, Jack. Richard Mainwaring and Derek Tate. Both just in.'

'*Okay.*'

'No match for Mainwaring from any of the victim's effects – clothing and such. Negative for touch-DNA, too, from swabs taken from the body.'

'And the brick used as the murder weapon?'

'As I already mentioned, touch-DNA found on its surface is days, maybe even weeks, old – most likely from builders working in the close. No match of Mainwaring's DNA there, either. The only thing more recent is acrylonitrile and butadiene residue.'

'And Tate?'

'Good news. His DNA matched specimens taken from Alice Cairns, Rachel Miller and Jan Ross. His genetic code fits all three.'

'So he's definitely our rapist?'

'No question.'

'That *is* good news, Ed. Thanks for getting back to me so quickly.'

'All part of the service, Jack.'

Knox ended the call just as Mason came into the room carrying two mugs of coffee. 'DI Murray?' she asked.

Knox smiled. 'Uh-huh. You and Kate were right; it's Tate.'

Mason's face lit up. 'Great,' she said, and took her iPhone from her handbag. 'I'll give Kate a ring.'

'You told me she lives this side of the town?'

'Yes, Relugas Road.'

Knox glanced at his watch. 'It's just after eight. She can meet you at Kilmaurs Grove and you arrest him.'

'And if he's already left for Bruntsfield?'

'Ring Torphichen Place. Have uniform pull him in.' Knox nodded to her phone, and added, 'That reminds me. I was wondering why Mainwaring hadn't got back to me. My iPhone battery's dead – I forgot to charge it last night.'

Mason took a swig of coffee. 'He probably left you a message,' she said.

'Aye, most likely. I'll charge it in the car on the way to the office.'

* * *

Knox was only five minutes from Gayfield Square when his iPhone showed enough power to let him check his messages. He tapped the voicemail icon and a moment later Mainwaring's voice came over the speakers:

"Inspector Knox: your phone's off at the moment, so I'm leaving a message. My mother says her driver retired on 17 May and his full name is James Scott Everett. I'd an idea he stayed in the Old Town but, as I said, didn't know exactly where. Now here's a coincidence: he lives at 11c World's End Close. I trust that helps. Thanks."

'Bit of an understatement,' Knox said out loud, then drove into the car park and exited the Passat.

As he entered the office, Hathaway and Fulton were already at their desks. He held up his iPhone, replayed the message, and addressed Hathaway: 'Mark, let me see that recording again.'

'The one from the clothes shop covering 11pm Monday till 12.30am Tuesday?' Hathaway replied.

'Yes.'

'Doesn't it show Everett walking his pooch?' Fulton asked.

'It does,' Knox said. 'At 11.33pm. I'm wondering if that's all it shows.'

Hathaway opened the file and spooled forward, then paused the recording and pointed to the image. 'Here we are, boss: 11.33pm. Everett walking down St Mary's Street with his Jack Russell.'

'Can you zoom in a little?' Knox asked.

'I think so,' Hathaway said, and clicked the mouse. 'Which part, boss?'

'There,' Knox said, pointing to the image. 'Give me a close-up of his hands.'

Hathaway clicked again and the section enlarged.

'I thought so,' Knox said, then turning to Fulton, he added, 'Notice anything?'

'I do,' Fulton replied. 'He's wearing nitrile gloves.'

Knox nodded. 'He told us he took the dog to a stretch of grass at the foot of the Pleasance,' he said. 'It's likely he had a plastic bag in his pocket to pick up its doings. The gloves'll be for extra protection.'

'Which he had on when he returned to the close?' Fulton said.

'Yes,' Knox replied. 'Until he got to the bins. Where he'd dispose of both.'

'Except he was still wearing them when Tuffnell and Mainwaring arrived?'

Knox dipped his head in acknowledgment. 'He must've been in the courtyard when Mainwaring knocked Tuffnell to the ground.'

'What happened then, I wonder?' Fulton said.

'Exactly what I intend to find out,' Knox said, picking up a phone on Hathaway's desk. 'I'm giving St Leonards a ring. Have uniform bring him in.'

* * *

Twenty-three Kilmaurs Grove was a mid-terraced villa near the foot of a cul-de-sac in the Priestfield area of the city. Mason had parked her Mini in a vacant space opposite and was opening the gate when a voice said, 'Can I help you?'

The detectives looked to the corner of the garden and saw a short, balding man kneeling beside a rhododendron bush.

Lyall took her warrant card from her pocket and held it up. 'Good morning,' she said. 'We're police officers. Detective Sergeant Lyall and Detective Constable Mason.'

The man put down a pair of secateurs and rose to his feet. 'Oh, I see,' he said. 'What can I do for you?'

'We're here to speak to Mr Derek Tate, sir. He's at home?'

'I'm Derek Tate,' the man said. 'What's it about?'

Lyall shook her head. 'Really? The man we'd like to speak to works with ATN Property Management at Bruntsfield.'

'Ah,' Tate said, shaking his head. 'Now I understand. You want my son. We've the same name – causes confusion sometimes.'

'Derek Junior, Mr Tate,' Lyall said. 'He's at home?'

'Afraid not. He left yesterday afternoon for a short break. He'll be gone until Monday.'

'Gone, sir?' Lyall said. 'Where?'

'The Isle of Skye, I think. Away to capture some landscapes. He's a keen amateur photographer.' Tate paused, his brow furrowing. 'May I ask why you want to see him?'

Lyall ignored the question. 'What time did he arrive home yesterday?'

Tate shrugged. 'In the early afternoon, I think.' He pointed to the door. 'Mary – my wife – will know exactly when. I was at the garden centre when he got in.'

'May we speak to her?'

'Of course.' Tate went to the door, opened it, and called out, 'Mary!'

They were joined moments later by a florid-faced woman whose hair was tied in a bun. 'Yes?' she said.

'Mary, these ladies are detectives. Called to see Derek. I said he'd gone on a trip to Skye. Told them I wasn't here when he arrived, only when he left.'

'Oh, I see,' she said. 'Would you like to come in?'

'If you don't mind,' Lyall said.

Mrs Tate opened the door and ushered Lyall and Mason into the hallway. 'The living room is on your right,' she said.

The detectives entered the room and she followed and waved to a sofa with a floral cover and matching cushions. 'Please,' she said. 'Take a seat. Would you like a cup of tea?'

Lyall took out her notebook and pen. 'No, thanks, we had some before leaving. Your husband was telling us he wasn't sure what time your son arrived home yesterday?'

'I had just finished lunch,' Mrs Tate replied. 'It would have been around one.'

'But you didn't expect him?'

'No. He usually arrives home in the early evening, sometimes a bit later.'

'What did he tell you?'

'That it had been quiet at the office and his manager, Mr Turnbull, had given him some time off – the remainder of Thursday, and Friday. Derek said he'd take advantage of it by driving up to Skye on a camping weekend. He packed his tent and other equipment in the boot of his car, together with his camera bag and tripod.

'I had some quiche leftover from lunch, and I laid out a plate for him before he went.' She paused and gave Lyall a searching look, then added, 'Look, I'm not quite sure why you're here. Is something wrong?'

'We've reason to believe your son is implicated in a series of assaults,' Lyall said.

Mrs Tate's face crumpled. 'No,' she said. 'That can't be true. Derek wouldn't harm anyone.'

Her husband, who had returned to the garden after his wife had shown in the detectives, appeared at the living room door. 'Something wrong, dear?' he said.

'Derek,' she said, still distraught. 'They're here to arrest him.'

'Arrest him?' Tate said. 'Why, in God's name?'

'We think he's guilty of a number of assaults on women,' Lyall said.

'Assaults? The rapes on young girls reported in the papers, you mean?'

'Yes.'

'Surely not,' Tate said. 'Derek's a kind, gentle lad. Not the type to do something like that.' He studied Lyall for a long moment, and added, 'You've proof of this?'

'Yes,' Lyall replied. 'We spoke to him yesterday at ATN Property Management's office at Bruntsfield. Before we left we took a sample of his DNA. The test result came back this morning. I'm afraid it was positive.'

'There's got to be a mistake,' his wife said.

'I'm sorry, Mrs Tate,' Mason said. 'Such tests are usually 100 per cent accurate.'

'Do you know your son's mobile phone number?' Lyall asked.

Mrs Tate got up from her armchair and retrieved a square of paper from the mantelpiece and handed it to Lyall. 'I always forget,' she said, 'so I write it down.'

Her husband picked up a cordless telephone from the top of a nearby sideboard. 'But his number's in our phone's memory,' he said. 'I'll give him a ring and ask him to speak to you.'

Tate held the phone to his ear for several moments, then shook his head. 'It's going straight to voicemail,' he said. 'He must have it switched off.' He replaced the phone on the charger and continued, 'You think I should get in touch with a lawyer?'

'That's up to you, Mr Tate,' Lyall said. 'But one would be provided anyway.' Then to his wife, 'It would be in Derek's best interests if we discover where he's located. Where on Skye did he say he'd be camping?'

'The Quiraing,' she said. 'Top north-east corner of the island.'

'Thank you,' Lyall said. 'If Derek should contact you in the meantime, you'll let us know? Like I say, it's in his own interest.'

'We will,' she said, shaking her head. 'I'm as anxious to speak to him as you are. I'm still sure it's been a terrible mistake.'

Chapter Twenty-one

Tate awoke just after nine, having slept on the couch. He gave himself a wash and had breakfast in a café in Hamilton Place, a short walk from the flat. The café had internet access, and he logged on and booked himself on a flight for Benidorm, leaving Edinburgh Airport at 11.15am the next day, using a prepaid credit card in Peter Jackson's name.

He returned to Raeburn Place, checked his watch, and saw it was almost eleven. He and Ray King had kept in touch, and two months earlier the timeshare property tycoon repeated his offer. Tate thought it prudent to keep his options open and told King he'd give it some thought.

He took out a Samsung pay-as-you-go mobile he'd bought the previous week, keyed in King's number, and pressed *call*.

The line took a few moments to connect, then he heard King's voice.

'Ray?'

'Derek? How are you, old cocker?'

'Fine, Ray. I promised I'd call back.'

'You've changed your mind?'

'Yes,' Tate said. 'Booked a flight with easyJet tomorrow. I arrive at 3.17pm your time, Benidorm Airport.'

'Champion, Derek. Glad to hear it. You've a place to stay?'

'Not really. Made up my mind on the spur of the moment.'

He heard King chuckle. 'Got yourself in deep with some woman again, eh? Don't answer that, son. None of my business.' A short pause, then, 'Yeah, you're okay. I've a flat lying spare in Carr. del Albir. You can crash there till we find you something more permanent.'

'I'm obliged, Ray. Thanks.'

'You're okay for cash?'

'I've a few hundred.'

'Good. Look, give me a ring when your flight gets in. I'll have someone meet you with the keys.'

* * *

'Did you notice the aftershave?' Mason said. She and Lyall were back in her Mini and heading into town.

Lyall shook her head. 'You've got me there, Yvonne,' she replied. 'No, I didn't. Where?'

'In the Tates' bathroom at the end of the hall. The door was open. A bottle sitting on a shelf above the sink – I was able to make out Knight Errant on the label.'

'Rachel Miller?' Lyall said. 'She mentioned her attacker wore a particularly pungent aftershave?'

'Uh-huh.'

'Another piece of the jigsaw slots into place,' Lyall said. She remained silent for a moment, then added, 'This photography trip to Skye. You think he told his parents the truth?'

'No,' Mason said. 'It has all the hallmarks of a false trail.'

'My thoughts exactly,' Lyall agreed.

'And his phone?' Mason said. 'Likely he ditched it after switching it off. He's bound to know we can locate its signal.'

'So he could be anywhere. Kitted out with camping gear, might not be easy to find.' Lyall checked her phone. 'I contacted the DVLA earlier. They've texted back with the make of his car and index number. I'll phone Central Control, Traffic Division. Have them do an automatic number plate recognition search on the motorways and check their archive for yesterday. See if we can get him that way.'

* * *

'Mrs Mainwaring phoned me just before your lads arrived,' Everett was saying. He had just been brought into Interview Room 2 by the arresting officers and was sitting opposite Knox and Fulton.

'She told me Richard had been arrested and released yesterday,' he continued. 'If I'd known that I would have handed myself in then.'

'Before you say more,' Knox said. 'I'd just like to make you aware that you're entitled to legal representation. We can hold off this interview until a solicitor is present.'

'No need,' Everett said. 'I'm done bottling this up. I need to make a clean breast of things.'

'Right,' Knox said.

'Okay if I start at the beginning?'

'Carry on.'

'You know I was Mrs Mainwaring's chauffeur?'

'Yes.'

'Well, I was actually employed by Mr Mainwaring. But drove his wife, too. They were top-notch employers – kind, fair; really nice people.'

'Mrs Mainwaring told us you retired in May?'

'Yes, I'd been with them twenty-eight years.'

'Go on.'

'Mrs Mainwaring's husband was a down-to-earth man, liked nothing more than discussing his investments on journeys to and from the law courts in Edinburgh. He used to say playing the markets was a little like horse-racing. It was simply a matter of studying form: an animal's track record was a reliable indicator of how it might perform over a series of races, and stocks were much the same.

'I'd never followed the horses myself – I'm not a betting man. But the older I got the more I wondered if investing in the markets might generate a top-up for my pension. One day I told Mr Mainwaring I'd saved in excess of £50,000. Asked if he could recommend a stock that might provide a bit of income. He told me he'd keep an eye out for any share releases that looked promising.'

'He recommended NewTech?'

'As it happened, no. By the beginning of this year he'd grown quite ill with bladder cancer. But he'd mentioned it to his wife, who was in the process of negotiating a deal with her brokers, Fairborough and Noble. By the time NewTech went public Mr Mainwaring had died. It was Mrs Mainwaring who took care of the investment for me.'

'And in April the company was taken to court and declared bankrupt?'

'Yes, we were devastated, of course. By then my investment had scattered to the four winds. Yet Mrs Mainwaring, who lost a great deal more than me, insisted I accept recompense of £10,000. She didn't have to do that. Needless to say, I was very grateful.'

'You began by saying Mrs Mainwaring phoned you?'

'Yes. Richard told her he'd been in an altercation with Tuffnell at the entrance to my close. She asked if I knew anything about it, and I told her yes. I also said I was unaware her son had been arrested.'

'Yes, you told us that,' Knox said. 'Regarding Monday night, do you want to tell us what happened?'

'I left the house about half eleven to take Sandy for his last walk of the day. My usual route; down St Mary's Street to the foot of the Pleasance. I waited while he sniffed around and did his business, then cleaned up after him and returned. I went to the back court, lifted the lid of one of the bins and dropped in the plastic bag with Sandy's excrement. I was about to take off the disposable gloves and dump them too, when I heard a commotion at the close entrance.'

'What time was this?'

'Near midnight.'

'*Okay*,' Knox said. 'What happened then?'

'I moved back into the close and saw two men arguing. Only after I heard him speak did I realise that one of them was Richard Mainwaring. It dawned on me that the other was Tuffnell after I heard Richard mention NewTech. I couldn't quite make out what else was said, then heard Tuffnell say "bugger off," at which point Richard threw a punch that felled him.'

'Did Tuffnell appear unconscious?'

'Yes. Richard waited a moment, but when Tuffnell didn't stir he turned on his heel and left. A moment later a taxi stopped, then I heard the door close and it drove off. I realised Richard must've hailed it.'

'Go on.'

'I slipped Sandy's leash and walked to where Tuffnell was lying. The dog got there ahead of me and began sniffing him. I realised he'd been drinking, as there was a strong smell of alcohol.'

'He got to his feet?'

'Yes. He looked at me as he stood and said, "Christ, another one."'

'"You remember me, then?" I said.

'"You were at court with the Mainwarings," he replied. "You're the chauffeur they bought shares for." He looked at his surroundings for a moment and added, "Where the hell's Mainwaring?"'

"'He's gone," I said. "Flagged down a taxi a minute ago."

'He scowled. "Blind-sided me with a lucky punch and fucked off, that it? What did he bring you along for – back up?"

"'I live here," I said.

'I don't know if he staggered then or attempted to push me. In any event, Sandy reacted: he barked, took one of the legs of Tuffnell's trousers in his teeth, and wouldn't let go. Tuffnell cursed, lashed out with his other foot, and caught Sandy's hindquarters. My dog yelped in agony and hirpled back to the courtyard, and began whimpering.

'I saw red. I looped the dog's leash over Tuffnell's neck and yanked him off his feet. I dragged him into the courtyard and told him to get up. Said I was about to give him a doing. Part of my anger was for Sandy, but a great deal of it had to do with losing my savings.

'He grabbed a brick lying near the bins and struck a blow at my leg. It caught me full on the shin and I dropped to the floor. He rolled towards me with a crazed look in his eyes, the brick still in his hand. He made a swing for my shoulder, which I just managed to avoid. I shuffled against a bin and he came at me again, aiming for my head. I dropped to my side as the brick thudded against the bin, and I saw another stone lying there.

'I picked it up and fought back. My blow caught him above the ear and he fell. I thought that was the end of it, but no: there was something manic about him. He rose, drew back his arm, and had another go... only missing me by inches. I realised then he was out to kill me – if I didn't get him first.

'We were much the same age, but I had an advantage: I was sober. He came at me a third time, swinging his arm in a wide arc. I jinked to the left, and the force of his effort caused him to lose his balance. He tripped, which was when I pounced. I took my brick and pummelled his head, not letting up until I was sure he was done for. I know it sounds callous, but at the time I felt I had to put an end to it. Like I said, it was either him or me.'

'The stone Tuffnell used against you,' Knox said. 'Where did he drop it?'

'Somewhere near the bins, I think. There's a few strewn about. Why?'

'Because if we can find that particular brick and prove Tuffnell handled it, it might make a difference to what you're charged with.'

'I'm sorry,' Everett said. 'I'm not sure I understand.'

'Culpable homicide versus murder,' Knox said. 'If we find a stone with Tuffnell's DNA it'll give credence to your statement.'

'Oh.'

'Okay,' Knox said. 'I'm going to defer charges for the moment. Our forensics people will take another look and see if they can locate the brick.' He nodded to a uniformed officer who stepped forward. 'You'll be remanded in custody, meantime.'

Chapter Twenty-two

'I just got off the phone with Turnbull,' Lyall was saying. 'The ATN Property Management's boss. He told us Tate left the office at lunchtime yesterday telling his secretary he was going to fetch a takeaway sandwich.'

Knox and Fulton had returned to the office, where the detectives were discussing both cases.

'But he went straight to his parents' house?' Knox said.

'Uh-huh,' Mason replied. 'Loaded up some camping gear and told them he was headed for Skye. We've been in touch with Traffic,' she continued. 'Asked them to check yesterday's ANPR recordings. Particularly the M90 and A9. See if that's really his destination.'

'He might be pulling a flanker?' Knox said. 'You think he's gone to ground?'

'Possible, boss,' Lyall said. 'Obviously we contacted Highland, who are currently checking the island. Nothing so far, though. But, of course, he could be headed in any direction.'

'Not necessarily A roads, either,' Knox said. 'ANPR won't pick him up if he's off the beaten track.' He shrugged. 'Okay. We'll just have to wait until Traffic gets back to us.'

Mason changed tack. 'Everett's admitted to killing Tuffnell?'

'Yes,' Knox replied. 'Though it's possible there's an element of self-defence.'

'He and Tuffnell fought?'

'So Everett says.'

'There's a scattering of broken house bricks at the locus,' Fulton said. 'According to Everett, there was a bit of a struggle. His dog went for Tuffnell, who kicked the animal's rump. Everett lost the place, threw its leash over Tuffnell's neck, and dragged him back to the courtyard–'

'Which would explain the marks Turley found on his neck,' Hathaway interrupted.

'Aye,' Fulton continued. 'Everett says Tuffnell was first to pick up a brick, then the fight began in earnest.'

'So the charge might be culpable homicide?' Lyall said.

'Might,' Knox agreed. 'I gave Murray a ring. He and Beattie are going to take another look this afternoon. They'll pick up any likely-looking bricks and run tests for Tuffnell's DNA.'

'And if they find it?'

'It'll back up Everett's statement,' Knox said. 'But even if I book him for manslaughter, it'll be up to the procurator fiscal to go with the lesser charge.'

The phone on Lyall's desk rang at that moment and she picked up the handset. 'Okay – thanks,' she said into the phone, then covered the mouthpiece and turned to Knox. 'Sergeant Simm at the front desk. He's about to transfer a call from Traffic. An Inspector Brennan. He promised to get back to me.' She flicked a switch. 'I'll put it on speaker.'

There was a momentary pause, then Brennan came on the line. 'Sergeant Lyall?' he said.

'Yes, sir.'

'Tate's car, a Honda Civic?'

'Yes.'

'One of our Traffic cars found it parked in Esslemont Road.'

'Here in Edinburgh?'

'Uh-huh. The officers checked the boot. Found camping equipment and a bag containing a Nikon D850 camera and tripod. There was nothing else, except a space in the boot between the tent gear and camera bag. Big enough for a holdall.'

'The only thing he's likely to have removed?'

'Looks that way.'

'Thanks, Inspector,' Lyall said. 'That's very helpful.'

'No problem,' Brennan replied, and rang off.

Knox thumbed his chin. 'What time did Tate leave his parents' house?'

'Mrs Tate told us two-thirty,' Mason replied.

'How long would it take to drive from Kilmaurs Grove to Esslemont Road?'

'Can't be more than a couple of miles,' Fulton said. 'Allowing for traffic, no more than ten minutes. But why Esslemont Road?'

'It's on a bus route,' Knox said.

Mason nodded. 'So, he's still somewhere in Edinburgh?'

'Of course,' Lyall said. 'He knew which of ATN's properties were vacant and had access to the keys. I'll give his boss another ring.'

She left the speaker on while she dialled the number, which rang three times before a woman answered, 'Good afternoon, ATN Property Management, Myra McKinnon speaking. How can I help you?'

'Hi, it's Detective Sergeant Lyall. May I speak to Mr Turnbull, please?'

'Hold on a moment, I'll put you through.'

There was a short silence, then the detectives heard Turnbull's voice. 'Hello again, Detective Sergeant. You've found Derek?'

'No. We think he may still be in Edinburgh. Do you have any vacant properties on your books?'

'A few, why?' Turnbull said, sounding surprised. 'You don't think Derek could be at any of those, surely?'

'It's a possibility, sir, yes. Would you mind checking for me?'

'Well, all the keys are in the front office and the cabinet there is locked. I'm the only one…' His voice trailed off.

'Mr Turnbull?'

'Sorry, yes. I just remembered. I've a spare set of keys for every property in a cabinet here in my office.'

'Did Tate know that?'

'I think so, yes.'

'Would you mind checking for me?'

'No. Hold on a minute.'

A few moments passed and Turnbull came back on the line. 'You're right,' he said. 'One of the keys isn't there. A flat we're currently renovating at 18a Raeburn Place.'

'You're sure it's the only key missing?'

'Yes.'

'Okay, sir. Leave it with us and we'll get back to you. Thanks for your help.'

Lyall put down the phone. 'You're right, boss. He took a bus.'

'A number 24 would take him from there to Stockbridge,' Fulton said.

'But why leave his car?' Mason said. 'Bound to know we'd find it sooner or later.'

'He took a chance,' Knox said. 'Because he doesn't intend staying long.'

'You think he plans on leaving the country?' Hathaway asked. 'Maybe he's booked a flight somewhere?'

'Very probable,' Knox said, then checked his watch. 'Okay – almost three. We'd better drive down there and prevent that from happening.'

* * *

It was the green Mini he recognised. He'd last seen it parked in Warrender Park Terrace, and it now came to a halt outside 18a with a VW Passat behind it. His suspicions were confirmed when the cop called Mason exited together with her older colleague.

He dodged into a doorway just as three males left the Passat: the driver, a man in his middle forties, and two others – a stocky man a decade older and a younger guy with red hair. The guy in his forties was obviously in charge: he beckoned to the others and the group came together. He nodded to windows above the stair entrance, then the older cop took a key from his pocket. He had the door open in seconds, then they went inside.

Tate cursed inwardly. He'd been in too much of a hurry – leaving the car where he did. He knew the cops would find it eventually, just not that soon. He should have parked in a side street where it was less likely to be discovered.

When they located the Honda they'd have contacted Turnbull, who would have told them the key to the flat was missing.

At least he'd been out when they arrived, which was lucky.

Feeling hungry, he'd walked to a nearby branch of Greggs, where he bought two packs of sandwiches and a couple of doughnuts. Afterwards, he stopped at a paper shop and bought a few cans of Coke and a copy of the *Evening News*. The grub would have kept him going until late the following morning, when he'd take a taxi to the airport.

Tate cursed again. *Damn!* A change of clothes was still in the holdall, together with toiletries.

Not to worry, he thought. I can get by without them. Fortunately, he still had his passport, together with credit and debit cards, and a print-out of his reservation, which he'd claim at the check-in desk. He'd more than £500 in notes, too, which he'd swap for euros at the airport's bureau de change.

He crossed the road and walked in the direction of Comely Bank, putting as much distance between himself and the flat, before patrols were alerted to carry out a search. He wasn't out of danger yet. He had to get out of the Stockbridge area, and quickly.

A taxi approached from the opposite direction, its hire light on. He stuck out his hand and it slowed, executed a U-turn, and came to a stop.

The driver rolled down his nearside window and leaned over. 'Where to, pal?' he said.

'West Princes Street. Will you go via Comely Bank?'

'Right you are. Hop in.'

Tate boarded the cab and the driver took a left into Comely Bank Avenue, a direct route to Queensferry Road and Edinburgh's West End. The cabbie had the option of going via Stockbridge and South Charlotte Street, as both routes were roughly equidistant, but that would have meant doubling back along Raeburn Place.

He asked the man to drop him at the corner of Hope Street and Princes Street, where he crossed the road and made for West Princes Street Gardens.

Even in the late afternoon, the city was busy with tourists, but he managed to find space on a bench overlooking the castle. He reached into his carrier bag, took out two packs of sandwiches and a can of Coke, and began to mull over his options.

No doubt they'd guess he'd fly from Edinburgh Airport. But they'd be looking for Derek Tate, not Peter Jackson. Any photograph in their possession would have been obtained from his parents. But, in the Peter Jackson image, he had a fair growth of beard and wore glasses.

He rubbed his chin as the thought occurred to him. Still not as much stubble as in the passport picture, but by tomorrow his beard would've thickened a little. He felt his inside pocket to confirm he still had the glasses, and was relieved to find that he had.

No, he felt sure his disguise would hold up. The false passport should see him pass through Border Control, as it had two years earlier. The women detectives who'd interviewed him at the office were unlikely to be at the airport, so any screening was likely be undertaken by local plods.

A dozen or so pigeons fluttered at his feet. Tate tore off a corner of a sandwich and threw it towards them. The birds scattered momentarily, re-gathering on the path, their heads bobbing at the bread.

His forced departure from Raeburn Place, though, left one problem unresolved: where to spend the night. Guest houses and hotels were a no-no – the cops were bound to be on the lookout. Public places, too, such as railway and bus stations were out, for exactly the same reason.

What did that leave? Parks? No, cops were bound to be keeping watch; anyone remotely resembling him would be stopped and made to prove their identity.

He finished the second sandwich, drank another Coke, and threw the empty wrappers and cans in a nearby rubbish bin. As he sat back on the bench a stiff breeze got up. He placed both hands into the pockets of his car coat and felt three sets of keys: two in the left pocket and one in the right.

The keys in the left he knew to be car keys and house keys. But those in the right he didn't recognise by touch. He withdrew his hand, studied the set for a moment, then realisation dawned: they were duplicate keys to Mason's flat in Warrender Park Terrace – he hadn't handed them in.

The cop had told him she was staying with her fiancé. She'd only popped in on Wednesday to discuss the terms of the lease and sign the contract. *Her flat is still vacant.*

Could he spend the night there? Of course he could. Safe from detection, courtesy of a member of Police

Scotland's finest. Tate gave a self-satisfied smile. *Oh, the irony.*

Chapter Twenty-three

'He must have been in the area somewhere,' Fulton was saying. 'Spotted us and skedaddled.'

He and the others had been at Raeburn Place for more than an hour, and the consensus was that Tate wasn't likely to return.

Knox pointed to a holdall near the sofa. 'I don't think he was planning on leaving today. There are toiletry items in the bathroom and a couple of towels. I think he'd have packed them if he was going tonight.'

'Any idea what his destination might be?' Mason asked.

'Not sure.' Knox thought for a moment, then addressed Lyall. 'Speak to his parents again, will you, Kate? Find out if he's been out of the country anytime in the last five years.'

Lyall nodded and moved away from the others, then highlighted a number and pressed *call*.

'Turnbull told us he'd been at ATN for two years,' Mason said. 'Maybe he worked abroad before that.'

'If he did, he'd have had a passport,' Fulton said.

'I agree,' Knox said. He indicated the holdall again. 'He only intended this as a short stay.'

Fulton nudged the bag with his foot. 'And it wouldn't have taken him long to pack.'

'My guess is he was planning to exit this weekend,' Knox said. 'Tomorrow or Sunday.'

'I'd say Saturday, boss,' Hathaway said. 'More flights.'

'Okay, we go on the assumption he plans to fly from Edinburgh tomorrow. That leaves him with the problem of where to stay tonight.' Knox turned to Hathaway, and added, 'Put the word out when we get back to the office, Mark. I want hotels and guest houses checked for one-night stays of men in his age group. Alert uniform to be on the lookout, too.' He paused. 'We've a recent photograph?'

Mason nodded. 'Took one on my iPhone when we interviewed him yesterday. He was talking to Kate at the time. He didn't see me take it.'

'Good,' Knox said. 'Relay the file to Communications, will you, Yvonne? I want it distributed to all forces.'

Lyall walked over and re-joined her colleagues. 'I've just spoken to Tate's mother,' she said. 'Two years ago he spent the summer in Benidorm, selling timeshare properties at a place called Playa de Altea.'

'Who was he working with?'

'She can't remember.'

'Doesn't matter. Yvonne, ask Communications to pass Tate's picture to the Spanish police. I've a hunch they'll have something on him. Mark, after you've done the alerts, check Saturday's scheduled flights for Benidorm.'

'Boss,' Hathaway said.

Knox glanced at his watch and saw it was just after five. 'Okay,' he said. 'Uniform can keep a watch here. We'll head back to the office and finish up, call it a day afterwards. I want everyone in at 7am sharp. I'm positive we'll have him in custody soon.'

* * *

It was almost dusk when Tate arrived. Public transport was busy with late commuters heading home, and he thought it safe to take a bus from the Mound to Marchmont Road, a short walk from Warrender Park Terrace. He approached Mason's block cautiously, but her distinctive green Mini was nowhere to be seen. He lingered at the edge of the Meadows opposite to make sure the coast was clear, then went up the stair and took out the keys. To be doubly sure, he thumbed her intercom buzzer, but received no reply.

He let himself in, stood for a moment, and listened for movement in the stair. Hearing nothing, he moved quickly up to the third floor and approached her door. Again he waited, but all was quiet. He opened the door and slipped inside, kicking aside an envelope on the hall floor.

Then almost immediately he heard it: the buzz of an alarm monitor. He remembered now: the system required a four digit PIN to be keyed in within thirty seconds or the alarm would go off.

When he left on Wednesday, Mason had given him a piece of paper on which she'd written the numbers. *What the hell have I done with it?* He flicked on the hall light and took out his notebook, then leafed through the pages and found her appointment entry. But he'd written nothing in the margin where he noted such details. He searched his pockets, to no avail.

The buzzing was almost cacophonous now – how many seconds had elapsed? He glanced at the read-out next to the keypad:

ELEVEN SECONDS REMAINING.

Wait! She said them out loud as she wrote them down. What the hell were they? Beads of sweat were beginning to form on his forehead as he struggled to recall.

All of a sudden he had it: *two-seven-four-two*. No... *two-seven-two-four*. He held his breath and keyed in the latter.

YOU HAVE ENTERED THE WRONG CODE. FOUR SECONDS REMAINING.

He cursed, keyed in *two-seven-four-two*, and heard a double beep and the display changed:

CODE CORRECT

Tate breathed a sigh of relief. He switched off the light and moved into the flat. You never knew, some nosy neighbour might see it and come calling. Or worse, pick up a phone and contact the boys in blue.

No, the flat would stay in darkness and he'd make little noise. He went into the living room, parked himself on the sofa, and took out his smartphone. He plugged in a set of earphones and clicked on Netflix. He'd watch a movie for the next couple of hours, after which he intended getting his head down.

* * *

'Which airline did Mark say had a scheduled flight to Benidorm tomorrow?' Mason was asking. She and Knox had just said goodnight to their colleagues and were standing outside the station entrance.

'EasyJet,' Knox replied. 'Leaves at 11.15am.'

'Did he check with the company?'

'Aye, nobody called Tate has booked, but that's neither here nor there. We expect him to be using a false name.'

'And a false passport to go with it?'

'No doubt. He's got form with the Spanish police. The *Guardia Civil* sent details in response to our query. Tate's wanted for the rape of a young woman a couple of years back. A girl called Sofía Estrella. She comes from Seville but met Tate in Playa de Altea. He fled the country then, so we've got to assume he used a false passport.'

'Which no doubt he still has?'

'I'm guessing so.'

Knox nodded to her Mini, then waved his car keys. 'Okay, we'll head on home. Fancy fish and chips tonight?'

'Make a change,' Mason said. 'We had a curry on Tuesday.'

'Will you do the honours, or will I?'

'I will,' Mason said. 'I have to stop off at my flat first and collect a new credit card. My old one's expired – they omitted to send me a replacement. I phoned the bank yesterday and they said they'd send out a new one. I forgot to ask them to post it to your place.'

'There's a chippy nearby?'

'Uh-huh, in Marchmont Road. I'll pick up the card and get the suppers on the way back.'

* * *

Tate was watching a film called *Danger Close*. The protagonists were in the middle of a firefight in a Vietnamese jungle and machine-gun fire and explosions filled his ears.

The living room, still in darkness, suddenly flooded with a shaft of light from the hallway. Tate immediately tore off the headphones and discarded the phone.

Someone's in the flat.

He rose to his feet and hastened towards the door. Glancing into the hallway, he saw Mason kneeling at the entrance. She was in the act of retrieving the envelope he'd knocked to one side.

He watched as she picked it up and tore it open, then saw her prise a plastic card from the letter inside. Mason put the letter back in the envelope, placed it on the hall table, and turned. She opened the door as if to leave, her hand on the light switch.

She stopped suddenly, glanced towards the alarm's keyboard, then closed the door again.

Of course. I disarmed the bloody thing.

Tate dodged back out of sight as she glanced towards the living room. He dashed to the sofa, reached inside his car coat, and retrieved his stiletto from an inside pocket.

He turned to see Mason framed in the doorway. There was a baton in her hand and the extendable section had been flicked into position. She reached inside, switched on the light, and saw him standing there.

'Derek,' she said calmly. 'What are you doing here?'

He clicked open the stiletto. 'Better put that cosh away,' he said. 'Else I'll cut you.'

'Of course,' Mason said, ignoring the threat. 'You had the keys to my flat. Needed a place to stay the night.'

'I'm not fucking joking,' Tate said. 'Drop that thing… now!'

'Come on, Derek. What's the point of making this worse than it is? Why not give yourself up?'

'Aye, right,' Tate said. 'And spend the next ten years in Saughton? No thanks.'

'The average sentence for the type of offences you've committed is only *seven* years, Derek. With good behaviour, you'd be out in four.'

'Which is four years too long, sweetheart. Now, are you going to move or do I make you?'

Mason indicated the knife. 'You haven't hurt anyone so far, Derek. Why start now?'

She took a step nearer.

'I'm serious,' he said. 'Another move and I'll have you.'

Mason took action, thrusting her baton hard at his right shoulder in an attempt to disarm him. Tate switched the knife to his left hand and parried the truncheon with his right. As the momentum of Mason's movement carried her forward, he made a swift and simultaneous jab with the blade.

The thin, razor-sharp shaft of steel penetrated several inches into Mason's chest. She gave a sharp gasp of pain, then slid to the floor and lay still.

Tate withdrew the knife, cleaned it with a tissue, and folded the blade back into the handle. He discarded the Kleenex, picked up his jacket, and edged past her inert figure.

Mason remained silent; her breathing shallow, almost imperceptible. Tate carried on to the front door and opened it and stood for a moment. Hearing no one, he descended the stairs, exited the tenement, and began to cross the Meadows.

* * *

Knox glanced at his watch: 9.07pm. He had last seen Mason more than two hours earlier. He'd tried calling, but the number had rung several times before switching to voicemail. She may have been delayed, of course, but why hadn't she rung to tell him?

She might have had an accident with the car. It was the only scenario he could think of which would have prevented her getting in touch.

He shrugged on his jacket and picked up his car keys, and was almost at the door when the phone rang. He turned, went back into the living room, and picked up. 'Knox.'

'Jack? Ron Warburton.'

'Sir?'

'I've just had a call from St Leonards.' A slight pause. 'It's Yvonne. She's been taken to the Royal Infirmary at Little France.'

'She's had an accident?'

'No, Jack. She's been stabbed.'

'Stabbed? Where did this happen?'

'At her flat. She was found forty minutes ago by an upstairs neighbour. The front door was open. The man thought he heard something and called out. Didn't get an answer and went inside. Found her at the entrance to the living room.'

Knox struggled to control his breathing. 'How bad is she?'

'Couldn't be much worse, Jack. She's lost a lot of blood.'

Chapter Twenty-four

Knox covered the two and a half miles from East Parkside to Little France in under seven minutes. He left the Passat at a parking space near the entrance and rushed to Accident and Emergency where the receptionist pointed him in the direction of Ward 116.

A woman in blue scrubs at the nurses' station looked up as he arrived. 'You're Detective Inspector Knox, Ms Mason's fiancé?' she asked. 'Reception told us to expect you.'

'Yes. How is she?'

'She's in theatre. The surgeon's draining fluid from her lungs and will try to close the wound.'

'How serious is it?'

'You know she lost a considerable amount of blood?'

'Yes.'

The nurse nodded. 'That's the main concern.' She pointed to a room at the opposite side of the corridor. 'If you'll take a seat in there. I'll have the doctor speak to you the moment the procedure's finished.'

The waiting room was empty, save for a dozen or so chairs positioned along the walls. A large table sat in the middle, on which lay a selection of magazines. A flat-screen television had been placed on a stand beneath a window. The set was tuned to a food channel, where chef Rick Stein was describing the process of garnishing sea bass.

Knox picked up the remote, muted the sound, and took a seat. He glanced at the television again. It was strange how everyday life appeared so at odds with the situation he found himself in.

How many folk had sat here, he wondered, with a loved one battling for life a short distance away? How many were able to find the calm to concentrate on a TV programme or read a magazine?

He heard movement in the corridor, and the door opened and two men wearing green scrubs entered the room. The older looked to be in his mid-forties, his colleague a couple of decades younger.

'Detective Inspector Knox?' the older man asked.

Knox stood. 'Yes.'

'I'm Gordon Wallace,' the older man said. 'My colleague is Alan Ballantyne. We've just come from theatre.'

Knox searched their faces. Wallace was impassive; serious and professional. But it was his young intern who told him what he wanted to know. Knox looked him directly in the eye; the young man was unable to hold his gaze.

'She didn't make it?' Knox asked.

Wallace gave a slight shake of the head. 'I'm sorry, Inspector,' he said. 'We drained the pleural cavity, but it was too late. The blood loss was massive, led to severe haemorrhagic shock. If she'd been admitted fifteen or twenty minutes earlier…'

'Can I see her?' Knox said.

Wallace nodded. 'Of course. I'll have our senior nurse take you.'

The doctors exited and Knox stood for a moment, then a middle-aged woman appeared. She had a Styrofoam cup in her hand, which she offered him. 'Inspector Knox? You're okay? You'd like some water?'

Knox accepted. 'Thank you.'

'Have a sip or two and I'll take you along.'

Knox downed the contents in one swallow. 'I'm ready,' he said.

He followed a short distance along the corridor, then the woman entered a room and clicked a switch. Fluorescent lights flickered on, revealing a small windowless room containing a curtained-off bed. The nurse went to one corner and took a chair, which she pulled over.

She drew the curtain back and said, 'I'll leave you in peace, Inspector. Take as long as you need.'

Knox sat on the chair and glanced towards the motionless figure.

Mason could almost have been sleeping. Her dark-brown hair hadn't lost any of its lustre, and her face, although pale, hadn't the waxen look he was all too familiar with.

Her arms lay outside the cover, and Knox saw her engagement ring had been removed from the hand closest to him, her left. No doubt they'd give it to him with her other possessions on the way out.

He reached out and took her hand in his. It didn't feel cold; it was as if the warmth of her personality was still there. He looked at the ring finger again. Had it been only three days since they'd discussed their Christmas Eve wedding?

Suddenly he remembered what she'd said about their planned honeymoon in Brisbane: *Hard to believe we'll be Mr and Mrs Knox by then.*

Knox kissed her ring finger. He felt tears prick his eyes and emotion swell in his throat.

He couldn't remember crying, not even at his mother's funeral. But here, in this tiny room, together with the body of the woman he'd hoped to spend the rest of his life with, he couldn't stop himself. He leaned closer, gripped her hand tighter, and his shoulders began to shake uncontrollably.

* * *

Tate covered the same ground he had on Monday when he'd followed Jan Ross, but in reverse: Middle Meadow Walk towards the junction of Lauriston Place.

Although fully dark now, it was still early – 7.30pm.

The encounter with Mason completely occupied his thoughts: the unexpected turn of events had thrown a bloody great spanner in the works.

He should've re-armed the system. If he'd taken that one precaution, she'd have taken the card and left, and he wouldn't be in this mess.

Damn! Why did she feel it necessary to have a go? He'd been cornered – if she'd only backed down when he threatened her with the knife.

No, she wanted to cuff him and call for back-up. But there was no way he'd allow that to happen.

Still, he hadn't meant to stick her: he thought the stiletto would have been enough of a threat.

She had guts, though, behaving as she did. Her last move was a total surprise; aiming the baton at his knife arm. Naturally, he'd reacted as anyone would – switching it to his other hand to counteract her move.

Trouble was, she'd acted faster and came closer than he anticipated. He thought the point of the blade would have nicked her, inflicted just enough damage to make her think again. But she kept coming. Before he knew it, the blade had sunk into her chest.

The wound looked bad. When she collapsed, he saw a helluva lot of blood. She hadn't made much of a sound afterwards. As he stepped past her to leave, he believed her to be breathing her last.

So, what did that make it… murder? They'd say it was, that was certain. Circumstances or no circumstances.

Yet was he really to blame? He'd given her plenty of warning. She ignored him, and he'd reacted.

But what did it matter now?

No doubt when she was found, there'd be a huge hue and cry. They'd be out in numbers, and nowhere would be sacrosanct. He had to find a place to spend the night, and soon, before the alarm was raised.

He crossed the pedestrian crossing at Lauriston Place and turned into Forrest Road. The centre of town was still busy, a good number of folk on the streets. And for that reason he still felt relatively safe.

But he wouldn't be for long. Late-night shoppers, workers and tourists would soon be heading home or to their hotels, leaving younger folk, who'd be out on the razzle.

Trouble was, young drunks often got into arguments and fights started. And fights attracted cops.

No, he didn't want to be out and about late. Particularly not this night.

He continued along Forrest Road, passing several shops which were still open, and came to the junction of Candlemaker Row and George IV Bridge. He stopped for a bus turning the corner, and his attention was drawn to two women on a short stretch of roadway leading to Greyfriars Kirkyard.

The women were American, both in their mid- to late-thirties.

'Very quiet in there, wasn't it, compared to outside?' he heard one say. 'You couldn't hear the traffic.'

'Yeah, really quiet,' her companion replied. 'And spooky.'

The woman's words echoed in Tate's head: *Very quiet in there.*

Greyfriars Kirkyard. Which part of the Old Town *could* be quieter? Or safer, come to that?

He recalled a school visit thirteen years earlier which had been part of a history project. He'd learned then that the kirk got its name from a Franciscan monastery dating from 1436. In 1602 the original Greyfriars Kirk was erected on the site, which had been rebuilt after a fire in 1845.

The actual graveyard, which occupied the top half of a slope leading to the Grassmarket below, was said to contain the bones of 100,000 dead.

Although open to the public twenty-four hours a day, few were prepared to venture there after dark, as the tombs and mausoleums were reputed to be haunted.

Where better to go to ground than in a remote corner of a graveyard? He recalled seeing a section at the foot of the cemetery where serried headstones screened a number of mausoleums.

He retraced his steps to a gift shop in Forrest Road, where he bought a Saltire baseball cap and two travel rugs, together with a bar of chocolate and a can of Irn-Bru. He had the assistant put these in a plastic bag and headed back towards the Kirkyard.

* * *

When Knox arrived at Gayfield Square the following morning, he was greeted by Hathaway and Lyall, who immediately offered their condolences. Knox thanked them and went to his desk, where he was intercepted by Fulton.

He gave Knox a sympathetic look. 'Mark phoned me late last night, boss,' he said. 'Told me about Yvonne. We're all gutted, but I know it's a helluva lot worse for you.' His eyes moistened, and he added, 'I'm sorry, Jack. I really am.'

Knox patted Fulton's arm. 'I know, Bill. Thanks.'

Fulton thumbed in the direction of Warburton's office. 'The DCI said to ask you to see him whenever you got in.'

Knox nodded and went to his boss's door, and knocked lightly.

'Come in,' Warburton said.

As Knox entered the DCI stood up and waved to a chair opposite. 'Please, Jack,' he said. 'Take a seat.'

As Knox did so, his boss added, 'How are you feeling? Get much sleep?'

'Some,' Knox replied.

'Look, Jack,' Warburton said. 'This stakeout at the airport this morning. Why not let me handle it? You've had enough to cope with.'

'Thanks, sir, but I want to be there when Tate's nicked. I owe Yvonne nothing less.'

'That's okay, Jack,' Warburton said. 'I understand.'

'Regarding Tate,' Knox said. 'ATN Property was contacted? Turnbull confirmed he failed to turn in the keys?'

'Yes,' Warburton replied. 'And DI Murray and DS Beattie went to the flat after Yvonne was taken to hospital. They found her baton lying on the living room floor. They think she was trying to apprehend Tate when he attacked.'

'We left the office together,' Knox said. 'She went back to pick up a replacement credit card.'

Warburton shook his head. 'I can't understand why he thought it safe to take refuge there.'

'Perverse thinking. Yvonne had asked ATN to handle the let. When he went to see her on Wednesday she told him she was living with me. After he gave us the slip at Stockbridge, he probably reckoned her flat would be the last place we'd look.'

Warburton nodded and gestured to the phone. 'By the way, I meant to tell you that the chief constable called. He asked me to offer his condolences and to tell you he intends recommending Yvonne for the Queen's Police Medal.'

Knox's answer betrayed a hint of sarcasm. 'Nice of him.'

Warburton gave him a placatory look. 'It's no consolation, I know, Jack.' He shook his head, and added, 'God knows, we're experiencing what no police officer wants to – the loss of a close colleague carrying out her duty. Doubly painful when that colleague is as dear as Yvonne was to you.'

'I shouldn't have said that, sir,' Knox conceded. 'I'm sorry.'

'You've nothing to apologise for.' The DCI flicked open a folder and studied the first page. 'Yvonne was born in Helensburgh? Her parents are deceased?'

'Yes,' Knox said. 'They drowned in a boating accident when she was fourteen. Yvonne was looked after by an aunt.'

'Her only living relative?'

'Yes. She still lives in Helensburgh. I phoned last night and she asked me to take care of the funeral arrangements. We agreed Yvonne would be buried here in Edinburgh. Sometime next week.'

'I see, Jack. You'll let me know the details later? The chief wants to pay his respects on the day, as do we all.'

Knox dipped his head in affirmation. 'Yes, sir,' he said. 'I will.'

Chapter Twenty-five

There had been a few tourists at Greyfriars Kirk, but the cemetery was empty. Tate had followed a meandering path to the foot of the incline, where the mausoleums were located. At the bottom he found the one he remembered – a gated tomb in a remote corner. It backed onto the boundary wall, and was hidden from view by tall headstones.

Tate went to the entrance and checked the gate which, although closed, gave a little when he tugged at it. He pulled harder. The gate made a rasping noise and moved again.

He glanced around to see if he'd been heard, but all was quiet. He took a firm grip of the bars with both hands and pulled a second time. The gate moved a little more, leaving a gap eighteen inches in width.

Tate took his bag and squeezed through. He entered the mausoleum and saw a sarcophagus to the left. Opposite was a stone shelf, which he assumed was where relatives sat when they paid their respects.

Tate removed one of the travel rugs from the bag, which he folded and placed on the shelf. He consumed the chocolate bar and drank the Irn-Bru, then lay on the first rug and covered himself with the other, and went to sleep.

* * *

He rested undisturbed, waking as the first shafts of light flooded the mausoleum. He folded the rugs and placed them back in the bag, then put on his thick-rimmed glasses and baseball cap and reversed through the gate. He strolled up to the church entrance, where he dumped the rugs in a rubbish bin, then exited the Kirkyard and walked in the direction of George IV Bridge.

It was a little after 7am, and the streets were relatively quiet. He crossed Candlemaker Row, where a solitary tourist stood at the edge of the pavement opposite the statue of Greyfriars Bobby. The man also wore a baseball cap, and looked to be in his late sixties. He had a camera to his eye and was taking a photograph. He pressed the shutter, then checked the screen at the rear.

Tate planned to hail the first passing taxi to take him to the airport, but decided to engage the tourist in conversation, as there was a possibility a police patrol might pass by first. With his baseball cap on he looked like a tourist, so it was likely cops would think them together.

'That's the new Canon 6D Mark II, isn't it?' he asked.

'Why, yes,' the man replied.

Tate noted he had an American accent. 'I thought so. Nice-looking camera. That's a 35mm 1.4 lens?'

'Uh-huh. Ideal for low light. You're a photographer?'

'Just an amateur,' Tate replied. 'I've a Nikon D850. Haven't got it with me today, though. I'm heading out to the airport. Business trip. Travelling light.'

The man nodded to the statue. 'Just came from our hotel to get a picture before we leave. It's an interesting story.'

'The dog?' Tate said. 'Yes. Held a vigil over his master's grave for fourteen years and was very well-known to locals. The then lord provost awarded him the freedom of the city.' Tate nodded to Greyfriars. 'He's buried just inside the churchyard.'

'Fascinating,' the man said. 'Wish I'd known sooner, I'd have paid the grave a visit. Have to make do with a photograph, I guess.'

Tate saw a taxi approach and put up his hand, but the hire light was off and the cab continued on.

'Did you say you were going to the airport?' the man asked.

'Yes.'

He pointed towards the opposite end of George IV Bridge. 'You're welcome to a ride if you want.' He glanced at his watch and added, 'I'm the tour organiser of a group of retired accountants from Philadelphia. We're staying at the Radisson, just along the road. Our contract hire bus is due to take us there in half an hour, 8am. It's a 32-seater, but there's only eighteen of us. Plenty of room.'

'I wouldn't mind, yes,' Tate said. 'That's very kind of you, Mr—?'

'Weiss,' the man replied. 'Joseph Weiss, but just call me Joe.'

'Thanks, Joe. My name's Jackson. Peter Jackson.'

Weiss extended his hand. 'Glad to know you, Pete.'

* * *

Knox's team at the airport were in place by 8am. Lyall, the only one to have seen Tate face-to-face, went to Police Scotland's control office, where a bank of CCTV monitors gave blanket coverage of the airport.

Knox, Fulton and Hathaway were positioned a short distance from the easyJet check-in desk: Knox near a Scottish Tourist Board information kiosk to the left of the easyJet check-in, Fulton and Hathaway at the other side, near the Air France counter. The detectives were in touch with each other via two-way radio on small waist-mounted transceiver devices.

When he arrived, Knox had been met by the officer in charge of airport security, Chief Inspector Simon Quinn. After Knox brought him up to date, Quinn asked, 'This Tate, you think he still has the knife?'

'Very likely, sir.'

Quinn looked concerned. 'We don't want to run the risk of him running amok on the concourse, brandishing the weapon and spreading fear and alarm. I've an armed unit at my disposal. It'd be safer to position them nearby.'

'I'd rather you didn't, sir,' Knox said. 'I'd like to keep as low a profile as possible. I'm sure myself and my team and I will manage to overpower him at the easyJet check-in.'

'But surely he'll recognise you? You mentioned he saw you at Stockbridge?'

'We think from a distance, sir, and only briefly. Detective Sergeant Lyall is the only officer he's seen up close.'

'Okay. If you're confident of taking him at the check-in desk, I'll let you go ahead. I'll instruct my men – including the armed unit – to stay in the background and give you a clear field. The moment that changes, though, or anything looks like it's getting out of hand, I'll instruct them to move. You understand, Inspector?'

'I do, sir, yes.'

* * *

It had been a great piece of luck, meeting the Yank. Tate had gone with him to the Radisson where their bus was waiting. There, Weiss introduced Tate to the other members of the tour group and they'd boarded, setting off for the airport just after eight.

As he exchanged small talk with Weiss and his wife, he realised it couldn't have worked out much better. The cops might be watching the airport, but he couldn't imagine they'd give much scrutiny to a bunch of elderly Americans departing for the States.

Once he'd passed any cops out front, it would be a piece of cake to separate from the group, go to the easyJet desk, and pick up his ticket.

He was glad, too, that he'd thought of the baseball hat – it added to his disguise. Together with the glasses and a two-day growth of beard, he looked much as he did in the passport.

There was always the woman detective, of course; Mason's sidekick. Except, when she saw him last, he'd been clean-shaven. If she *was* there, she'd be hard pressed to recognize him now.

And the cops couldn't know which flight he was booked on, if any. He reckoned they'd cover the airport, but only as a precaution. There was one thing for sure: they wouldn't be looking for a man called Jackson.

The coach cruised to a halt at the drop-off point at the main terminal building. The Americans at the front exited and went to the rear as the driver opened the luggage compartment and began unloading their bags.

Tate exited with Weiss and watched his wife walk to a trolley park near the entrance. Two uniformed policemen flanking the doors looked on with disinterest as the Americans began milling around the rear of the coach as the driver took out their bags.

Weiss nodded to a couple of large brown leather cases as his wife rolled a trolley towards the baggage hold. 'These are mine, driver,' he said.

Tate glanced back at the cops, who remained impassive. No sense in tempting fate, he thought.

'Here,' he said, reaching for the Weisses' luggage. 'Let me get these for you.'

As he placed them on the trolley, Weiss said, 'That's mighty nice of you, Pete.'

'Least I can do,' Tate replied, nodding to the entrance. 'Anyway, my plane doesn't leave for a couple of hours. Which flight are you on?'

'American Airlines for Philadelphia,' Weiss replied. 'Leaves at 10.10am. Gate 11. We've to check in from 9am onwards.'

'Okay,' Tate said. 'Like I said, I've no luggage. I'll take these to the desk for you.'

'Real kind, Pete. Appreciate it.'

Tate pulled the baseball cap over his forehead and pushed the trolley past the police officers and into the main concourse. The Weisses and the others in their group followed.

'There we are,' his wife said, pointing to an overhead information board. 'Gate 11. We need to go to the right.'

* * *

Back in the control room, Lyall was watching arrivals. Her attention was drawn to a group passing through the main entrance who were headed in the direction of Gate 11. One particular individual stood out – a younger man amongst a group of elderly tourists. He was pushing a trolley and was flanked by a man and woman, but there was something familiar about him.

She turned to the civilian operator alongside her and pointed to the screen. 'The three people heading that group,' she said. 'Can you get me a close-up?'

The operator, a young man called Dave, reached over and pushed a joystick-like lever. 'Sure,' he said.

The camera zoomed in on the group. Lyall studied them for a few moments, but the man pushing the trolley continued to keep his head down.

'Are we seeing this on an overhead camera, Dave?' Lyall asked. 'There isn't a monitor that'll give us a view nearer ground level?'

Dave indicated a screen on their left and turned a knob on the main control panel. 'We have one at the side of WH Smith. They'll pass there in a second or two.'

Lyall glanced at the screen as the man pushing the trolley approached the camera's location. The couple were laughing, as if their companion had said something funny. Then he looked up, and she saw his face. He hadn't shaven in a while and was wearing thick-rimmed spectacles, but there could be no mistake: it *was* Tate.

Lyall immediately reached for her radio and pressed the *transmit* button. 'I've got him, boss,' she said.

'Where?' Knox replied.

'He came in the main gate opposite you, then veered off to the right. He's with a group of tourists, headed to the Gate 11 check-in. Unshaven. Wearing thick-rimmed glasses and a dark-blue baseball cap.'

'Which airline?'

Lyall looked at Dave, who said, 'American Airlines.'

'American Airlines,' Lyall repeated. 'A group of older folk. He must've met them in town. He's helping one particular couple with their luggage.'

'Safety in numbers, eh?' Knox said. 'Not to worry. He'll head back to the easyJet desk afterwards.' Knox paused, then added, 'Where exactly is he now?'

Lyall repeated Knox's question to Dave and he flicked to another monitor.

'At Gate 11 together with the Americans,' she said. 'Wait. He's just shaken hands with the couple he came in with… he's turning… I think he's heading back towards you.'

'Good,' Knox said. 'Keep an eye on him, will you, Kate? Let us know the minute he arrives at the main concourse. We'll be waiting for him.'

* * *

Tate arrived at the easyJet counter. A man in front had just been served, and Tate moved forward.

'Good morning, sir,' the receptionist said.

'Morning,' Tate replied, handing over a print-out of his reservation. 'Peter Jackson. I'm booked on the 11.15 flight to Benidorm.'

'Fine, sir. May I see your passport?'

Tate handed over his passport, which the woman took and handed to her colleague, an older woman with grey hair. The woman scrutinised it for a moment, then Tate saw her eyes flick towards a couple of men standing next to the Air France check-in a short distance away.

An older man and a younger man with red hair.

Suddenly it dawned on him: the detectives he'd seen in Stockbridge.

The older woman stood up. 'Would you mind waiting, sir?' she said, holding up the passport. 'Border Control are doing a check this morning, we won't keep you a moment.'

He glanced again at the detectives, who had begun walking in his direction. *They're on to me! The game's up!*

Tate moved away from the desk, reached into his jacket and took out the stiletto, flicked it open and brandished it at the detectives. 'Stay where you are,' he said. 'Another step and you'll get a knife in the gut.'

Knox, standing beside the tourist information kiosk, heard Quinn over the radio: 'It's gone south, lads,' he said. 'Get ready to move in.'

Knox glanced towards the main entrance, where arrivals were still streaming into the concourse. Any one of their lives could be in danger.

'No, sir, don't,' he said quietly into his cuff microphone. 'Tate will attempt a retreat and might take a hostage. Have your men seal off the door, then send three or four officers to back up my men. I want his attention focussed on them. I'll get in behind and disarm him.'

'Okay, Knox,' Quinn said. 'The entrance is sealed. But you've only one chance. Cock it up and I'll send in the armed squad.'

'Understood.'

Knox saw the entrance doors close and four uniformed officers take up position outside. A further six policemen entered the concourse behind Fulton and Hathaway and advanced towards Tate, who was now looking increasingly desperate. He waved the knife in their direction and repeated his threat. 'Stay where you are. I'll gut the first bastard who comes near me.'

Knox spoke into his microphone again. 'Bill, Mark and those at their rear. Keep him facing you. I'm going to attempt to come in behind.'

Fulton nodded, then he and Hathaway took another step forward. The other officers followed suit.

Tate glanced in the direction of the easyJet kiosk, and Knox realised what was on his mind: he was going to vault the check-in desk and take one or both women hostage.

Knox didn't wait for that to happen. He rushed in at Tate's back, grasped his knife arm by the wrist, and yanked it up hard behind his back. He heard a distinct *snap*, and the knife dropped.

'You prick!' Tate screamed. 'You've broken my arm.'

'Consider yourself lucky,' Knox said quietly. 'If I had my way, I'd have broken your fucking neck.'

* * *

Tate was taken to Gayfield Square Police Station where he was charged with murder, three counts of rape and one attempted rape, and remanded in custody.

The detectives were back at their desks when a call came in from forensics.

'Liz and I searched World's End Close again,' DI Murray told Knox. 'Near the bins. We found three likely-looking fragments of brick and analysed them. One had Tuffnell's DNA on it.'

'So, Everett was telling the truth,' Knox said. 'Tuffnell did attack him.'

'Looks that way, Jack.'

'Did you let the procurator fiscal know?'

'Yes,' Murray replied. 'Just got word back this morning. They're going with a charge of culpable homicide.'

'Good to hear.'

'By the way, Jack, about Yvonne… neither Liz nor I have had a chance to express our condolences. We're devastated at what happened.'

'I appreciate it, Ed. Thank you.'

'Okay, Jack. Take care.'

Warburton exited his office as Knox ended the call. He checked his watch as he walked over. 'Twelve-thirty,' he said to Knox. 'There's nothing else?'

'Nothing active, sir, no.'

'Okay. We were up early. We can call it a day.'

'Thank you, sir,' Knox said. 'I think we're all pretty much beat.'

Lyall and Hathaway were first to take their leave. They said their goodbyes and left the office, and a few minutes later Knox and Fulton followed. They descended the stairs to the reception area, where a young man in his early thirties was talking to the desk sergeant.

He glanced up as Knox passed and said, 'Detective Inspector Knox?'

'Yes,' Knox replied.

'You don't recognise me, sir?' he said. 'Robin McAllister. I was a probationer DC here at Gayfield three years ago.'

Knox looked at McAllister again. 'Oh, yes, I remember now. Weren't you transferred to Torphichen Place after you qualified?'

'That's right, sir. I'm a full DC now.' He nodded to the desk sergeant. 'I was just passing and decided to drop in and say hello to Sergeant Lowrie. He's my uncle.'

Knox glanced at the sergeant, who winked. 'Just telling him to mind his Ps and Qs, boss,' Lowrie said jokingly.

'How are you finding the job?' Knox asked McAllister.

'Worked on quite a few cases, now, sir. Several I've helped to clear up.' He shrugged. 'Others, well… things go wrong. Things don't always pan out as you hope.'

Knox nodded. 'That's the job, Robin,' he said. 'Anyway, nice to see you again.'

He exited the door then together with Fulton, who took out his car keys and indicated a Vectra parked across the road. 'Okay, boss, I'm off home. See you on Monday?'

'See you Monday, Bill. Have a nice weekend.'

Knox crossed to his car and activated the remote locking. As he returned the keys to his jacket, he felt a small metal object deep in the pocket – Yvonne's engagement ring. He'd put it there when he left the Royal Infirmary the previous night.

He took it out and glanced inside: *Yvonne* and *Jack* were engraved at either side of a heart, together with the inscription *Cuffed Together Always*.

Knox shook his head in sorrow as McAllister's words came back to him: *Things don't always pan out as you hope*.

The End

List of characters

Officers based in Edinburgh:

Detective Inspector Jack Knox – head of the Major Incident Inquiry team based at Gayfield Square Police Station, Edinburgh

Detective Sergeant Bill Fulton – Knox's partner, second member of the Major Inquiry Team

Detective Constable Yvonne Mason – third member of the Major Inquiry Team

Detective Constable Mark Hathaway – fourth member of the Major Inquiry Team

Detective Chief Inspector Ronald Warburton – senior detective at Gayfield Square Police Station

Detective Inspector Edward (Ed) Murray – forensics officer with the Scottish Police Authority (SPA)

Detective Sergeant Elizabeth (Liz) Beattie – forensics officer and Murray's assistant

Detective Sergeant Kate Lyall – sexual offences liaison officer

Alexander Turley – pathologist

Chief Inspector Simon Quinn – officer in charge at Edinburgh Airport

Other characters:

Jan Ross – third rape victim

Rachel Miller – second rape victim

Alice Cairns – first rape victim

Adrian Tuffnell – murder victim

James Everett – the man who found Tuffnell

Sir Michael Fairborough – MD Fairborough and Noble

Maxwell Denison – major NewTech investor, deceased

Susan Dalrymple, née Denison – investor's daughter

Edward Denison – Susan's brother

Arthur Lawson – Edward Denison's friend

Jason and Ross Wylie – NewTech directors

Brigadier Reginald Coutts – NewTech investor

Mrs Frances Mainwaring – NewTech investor

Richard Mainwaring – Frances Mainwaring's son

Derek Tate – ATN Property Management representative

Mr Turnbull – ATN Property Management boss

Ania Joscowski – ATN Property Management lessee

Lidka Nowak – ATN Property Management lessee

Ray King – Tate's boss in Benidorm

If you enjoyed this book, please let others know by leaving a quick review on Amazon. Also, if you spot anything untoward in the paperback, get in touch. We strive for the best quality and appreciate reader feedback.

editor@thebookfolks.com

www.thebookfolks.com

MORE FICTION BY ROBERT McNEILL

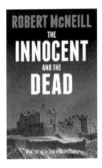

The Innocent and the Dead (Book 1)

One girl is found dead – strangled in the woods. Another, the daughter of a rich, well-connected businessman, is kidnapped. Unassuming detective, Jack Knox, must solve these two cases. But the Edinburgh crime-solver will have a hard time getting his superiors to accept his unconventional methods. Will he gamble too much?

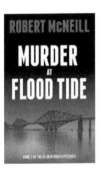

Murder at Flood Tide (Book 2)

When a young woman's body is found, the nature of her killing leads detectives to believe the murderer may strike again soon. The race is on to find him, but he has covered his tracks well. DI Jack Knox's investigation is impeded by a disgruntled officer from another force. Can he solve the case and collar the culprit?

Dead of Night (Book 3)

When a philandering French college lecturer is killed and unceremoniously dumped in a canal, DI Jack Knox soon discovers there is no shortage of spurned lovers and jealous husbands who might have done it. He sets about collaring the culprit, but will his efforts be thwarted by unfair complaints made about the investigation?

A View to Murder (Book 5)

When a student is found dead in the crags in Holyrood Park, DI Jack Knox must make sense of her friends' conflicting stories about the events that led up to her death. But his boss risks putting a spanner in the works when Knox is asked to act as a go-between in a deadly drugs sting.